how you lose

how you lose

J. C. Amberchele

A NOVEL IN STORIES

CARROLL & GRAF PUBLISHERS • NEW YORK

HOW YOU LOSE

Carroll & Graf Publishers
An Imprint of Avalon Publishing Group Inc.
161 William St., 16th Floor
New York, NY 10038

Copyright © 2002 by J. C. Amberchele

First Carroll & Graf edition 2002

Book design by Michael Walters

The following stories were previously published: "Melody" in *Oasis* and
Doing Time: 25 Years of Prison Writing; "Old Max" in *Prison Life*; "Wildflowers"
in *Short Stuff Magazine*; "Where Fathers Go," "Passing Through," and
"Orphan Ranch" in *The Beachcomber*; "So I Told Him" in *Writers' Forum*;
"How You Lose" in *Quarterly West*; "The Ride"in *Fortune News* and "Mel" in
Fortune News and *Doing Time: 25 Years of Prison Writing*; "The Interview"
in *Blue Mesa Review*; "State Hospital" in *Wind Magazine*; and "Knee High"
in *Portland Review*.

Library of Congress Cataloging-in-Publication Data is available.

ISBN: 0-7867-0997-9

Printed in the United States of America
Distributed by Publishers Group West

For my daughter

And for my son, who died in prison, too young.

contents

Melody   1

Hardly Friends   19

Old Max   41

Wildflowers   49

Where Fathers Go   67

So I Told Him   75

How You Lose   85

The Ride   95

The Interview   111

Do I Know You?   139

Passing Through   155

Orphan Ranch   163

State Hospital   175

Knee High   197

Mel   209

how you lose

Melody

Mel is standing on the curb in front of her father's house, digging in her knapsack for the key and wondering how she could have misplaced it; or why she has misplaced it; wondering if maybe she has misplaced it on purpose. She is aware of the dream and thinking: I'll be a sibyl, a seeress. I'll see halos and auras, I'll predict the future. . . .

It is noon and the cab has just dropped her off, and she's had a headache since this morning when she left Omaha.

"I'll find keys," she says out loud, surprising herself with her sarcasm, and immediately remembers an inside pocket on her windbreaker.

The house has been empty for a year. It is brick and stone, three stories under a red tile roof. There are turrets at the front corners, three-quarter round with bay windows on all floors, medieval structures that to Mel have always seemed an architectural afterthought. Out front on the lawn is the stocky red juniper her father planted before she was born,

and at the curb, towering over the street, the roots so effort-
lessly shrugging the pavement aside, is the ancient sycamore
that has been around longer than the houses on the block.
The hedge separating the yard from the neighbor's is frantic
with growth, but the lawn has been mowed—the real estate
company has seen to that—although the first thing Mel
noticed from the taxi was that no one had taken down the
blue window awnings this past winter, and now they look
faded and sad. Sad windows and sad gray walls, the welcome
mat missing from the front steps, ivy gone wild and snagging
the rain gutters, the chimney fascia spilling its rust down the
wall overlooking the driveway. Her father's castle, his crum-
bling fortress in the middle of the block.

On the porch, knapsack harassing her shoulder, Mel fingers the key from her jacket and aims it at the lock, noticing
as she does that her hand is trembling.

She is here to meet the woman from the real estate company. There is a buyer for the house, and a good offer. Paul,
Mel's brother in Omaha—where Mel has spent the last year
recovering—has come to Denver twice this month to arrange
the sale, and Mel didn't actually have to return. But the deal
didn't include the furniture, room after crowded room of
turn-of-the-century tables and chairs, antique wall hangings
and rugs, thousands of knickknacks—and ostensibly Mel has
come for this: to sell or store the furniture, or as she told Paul
before she left, to check her room one final time, to see if
there is anything she wants to keep.

Mel closes the door behind her, but then swings it open again because the air in the hallway is stale. She eases her knapsack to the floor and looks down the length of the narrow room. To Mel the hall has always been the unfriendliest room in the house, a dim passageway of hardwood floors and empty walls, so unlike the other rooms. There are heavy sliding doors, closed now, to the parlor on the left and the dining room on the right, and farther along there are single doors to the den and to the closets under the stairwell. Toward the rear of the house is an entryway to the kitchen, and next to it, another door—the service stairs, a metal spiral in a narrow shaft from basement to roof.

Which was how he got to them, so quietly, she and her father light sleepers who would have heard the familiar creak of the staircase in the hall, the groan of the wooden banister.

She awoke with the barrel of the gun pushed between her lips, icy metal against her teeth, the reading lamp turned toward her and shining in her eyes. He wore a ski mask, a ratty blue parka that rustled as he moved. All she could think was that she was naked beneath the covers. He drew the gun from her mouth and pointed it at her head and with the other hand shoved a note in her face—so as not to reveal his voice?, she wondered—squinting, trying hard to focus on the words. The safe, it said. Where is the safe, and what is the combination?

But there was no safe. She hesitated, and then couldn't speak. He motioned for her to sit up. She did, spilling the covers to her lap. Curiously, she wasn't afraid. She felt her heart race, felt her skin turn cold; her eyes stung from the brightness of the bulb, and what puzzled her was that she knew this man would probably kill her, and yet she wasn't afraid, as if in her mind there wasn't room or even time enough for fear.

He took her arm and pulled her from the bed, spun her around, and jammed the gun in her hair—her wild hair, springy curls out past her shoulders—and pushed her to her father's room down the hall.

Mel opens the sliding doors to the dining room. Nothing has changed. The walls are cluttered with eighteenth century engravings and elaborately framed mirrors. The Queen Anne dining set, the china case, look recently polished; the crystal glassware and figural silver are displayed exactly as they have always been.

She walks into the kitchen. The refrigerator door is open; the light is off. She closes the door and lifts the phone off the wall and holds it to her ear, knowing there will be no dial tone. Except for her bedroom, this was her favorite part of the house, here at the oak table in the breakfast nook where she'd read or do her homework, the afternoon sunlight angling through the bay windows. By the time she was twelve, she was mostly alone here: Her father could no longer afford the maid, and by then her brother had left home permanently. And so after school she would bring her books to the table by the window, and then with cookies or maybe a cake in the oven, she would dream up salads or fix casseroles that too often her father wouldn't show up to eat. Even so, the idea of something ready on the stove or warm in the oven was a comfort to her.

Mel hangs up the phone and, returning to the hallway, hears a car pull up out front—and knows it is Beth, the real estate lady who is selling the house. This wasn't Mel's idea. It was Paul who had called Beth from the airport. But then in a way it was Mel's idea because it was she who had insisted on coming back, and selling or storing the furniture was the handy excuse, something Paul would understand. Paul who had ignored her all her life and who now acted as though he needed her, as though he needed to protect her.

Mel walks to the front door. Beth steps out of her shiny car and looks up at the giant tree spreading high above her, and somehow at that instant Mel realizes that the new owners, whoever they are, will cut it down, will decide it is too old and too big for the neighborhood.

"Such a lovely tree," Beth calls from the curb. She wears a white suit with low heels to match, a floppy spring hat that Mel thinks is silly. Approaching the porch she says, "I hope it survives. You know, this Dutch elm disease is rampant here."

"It's a sycamore," Mel says, and Beth shrugs and flips a hand in the air as if to say, Sycamore, elm, what's the difference?

Beth is a retired housewife, in her late forties, Mel decides. Her nose is too long and her mouth too wide, but other than that she is attractive in a motherly way. Paul has been in touch with her since last fall, ever since he and Mel agreed to sell the house. Paul, twenty-nine and recently divorced, is ten years older than Mel; he is a dentist in Omaha where he lives in a boxy suburban neighborhood and cares for his two young sons. For the past eleven months, ever since she left the hospital, Mel has been recovering at Paul's, taking care of the boys when she can. Paul has made trips to Denver about the house, but Mel couldn't return, not until she was ready. And then one night when he was away she dreamed a crazy dream, a dream similar to the recurring nightmare, but different because this time she knew she was dreaming; like a spectator at a film, she saw herself return to her father's house, watched as she moved from room to room reliving the horror of that night. Abruptly the dream shifted to a distant future in which she had arrived at an unknown faraway place, and there in her mind had grown numb and therefore comfortable and as a bonus had acquired strange mental powers— she could read people's auras, she could see their lives unfolding, minute by minute—a future in which she existed in the same spatial dimensions as everyone else and yet in a time slightly ahead so that even her own days were predictable, a future in which the nightmare of the past had ended, had vanished as, in a sense, she herself had vanished.

The man snapped the overhead light on, and her father sat up as they entered the room. He sat up blinking. There wasn't much else he could do, not with the gun at her head, naked as she was and with the man gripping her neck from behind. The man pulled her father out of bed, motioned for them to lie on the floor, facedown. He grabbed a blanket and tossed it over her, a thing that surprised her, but then he knelt above her and yanked the blanket down and forced her hands behind her back where he taped her wrists, moved to her ankles and taped them also, then started on her father. And her father kept asking, why?, and who was he?, and what did he want?, over and over, with the tape tearing, screeching in Melody's ear. But the answer, when it came, was only the note, this time held low to her father's eyes. Where was the safe? What was the combination?

But there was no safe. Her father told him. There never was a safe, not in this house. On the dresser—take the wallet, the watch—take the TV, anything. Just don't hurt them.

And Melody kept thinking: He won't hurt us, he only wants money, he'll take the wallet and leave.

He began with the paintings on the wall, tore them off one by one and threw them to the floor, then moved to the closet, ripped the clothes out, and pulled all the boxes off the shelves. No safe. He stopped, chest heaving, and Melody could feel his anger, could almost see the air around him boil with rage. He stood above them for a moment, then suddenly grabbed her father by the hair and pressed the gun to his forehead . . . and Melody waited, wanting desperately to be afraid, wanting fear to release her, to feel it as a poison in her blood, pumping into her mind, pumping everywhere at once.

There was a life insurance policy, a few dollars in a checking account, a trust fund for her college tuition. Paul sold the car and gave her half the money, but she gave it back as monthly rent. Even after the hospital bill, her half of the insurance policy and the money from the house would be more than enough.

As for the trust fund, her father had never mentioned it. But that was like him, not to tell her. A man who had lost his wife when Mel was born, he was silent and brooding, tall, with sunken eyes and permanently hunched shoulders; he rarely told her anything. There were entire days when he didn't speak to her, so that she grew up trying too hard, hoping to replace not only his loss but her own. There were financial problems. Eventually he sold the printing company that had been his grandfather's and his father's and took a job in the press room at the *Denver Post*. And Mel had finished high school and had attended her graduation ceremony alone, had spent a year after that working odd jobs and hanging around the library downtown—and he hadn't said a thing about a trust fund.

"You know what I like about this place?" Beth says. "It's so quiet." She pats the wall next to the front door. "It's so solid."

Mel considers smiling, but isn't sure it won't come out as

a frown. Although Beth is right: The house is quiet. Mel's paternal grandparents had lived and died here before she was born; they were, as her mother and her mother's parents were, more of the silent family she never knew. Growing up, Mel embraced the silence, took it for her own, but Paul came up angry, hating this house and leaving as soon as he could. Now Mel isn't sure what to think. This was never a happy place, never a place for a child, really, but it is all she knows. And now she must forget it. She must walk through it, room by room, erasing it from her mind.

She slides open the doors to the parlor. The furniture is untouched—the sofa and love seat by the fireplace, the octagonal table in the turret bay, the Estey pump organ against the wall. There are too many tables: coffee tables and end tables and corner tables, all busy with knickknacks that have never meant a thing to her, but to which she now feels an unwelcome attachment, knowing they are hers to dispose of.

"Try the sofa by the fireplace," she says to Beth. She is aware of having acquired a short fuse: Since the hospital she has found it difficult to listen to her brother complain about his divorce, and today in the taxi on the way from the airport she snapped at the driver when he tried his small talk. Mel doesn't wish to be rude to Beth, but neither does she feel a need to explain. It is simply that she must do this alone. "I'll be back," she says.

She climbs the stairs to the second floor, crosses the balcony, and enters her bedroom. The room is sunny; the drapes have been drawn from the window overlooking the back-yard, probably by her brother on his recent visit. Here, there is a thin layer of dust over everything: the massive headboard on the bed, the heavy walnut dresser with the teardrop pulls, the books piled on her desk and floor. It was never a girl's room, never frilly, although when she was six her father relented and replaced the antique wallpaper with Pooh char-acters: Owl and Eeyore and Christopher Robin, Pooh and Piglet following in circles the multiplying tracks of a Woozle—they have faded now, and the paper is brittle, about to peel from the walls.

She stops at the window. The lawn in the backyard is patchy, blemished with debris brought by the winter wind, and the dogwood tree, bursting with hundreds of clusters of brilliant white flowers, seems delirious, abandoned to nature. Beyond the fence there is the wide expanse of the neighbor's lawn, and across the street, the country club where as a child she would spend her weekends. Alone on winter Sundays she would test the frozen creek, hike the empty golf course that became her private estate; the trees she would climb were make-believe houses where she'd perch in her heavy coat like a silent bird, watching frosted cars glide by on a nearby avenue. She was a tomboy; she was more a boy than a girl. She thought of herself as odd and graceless and at fault, and with her brother so much older and her father hardly home even when he was, there was no one to tell her differently.

Mel turns and leaves the bedroom, but stops just outside the door. She is suddenly lightheaded, dizzy. She is fine, she tells herself. She has come this far; she can go on. She takes a breath and steadies herself with a hand against the wall, walks to her brother's room and looks in, then continues around the stairwell toward her father's room. This is why she has returned. She has forced herself to this room because she believes in the dream. She has rehearsed this a hundred times in her mind; she is convinced she can walk in and walk out and in that fleeting turn bring it all back—everything: the senselessness of it, the horror, the fear that would never come. And then walk out and forget it, forget this room altogether . . . or perhaps remember it as it had always been, so perfectly ordinary: his robe hanging on the back of the closet door, the collection of antique paperweights on the roll-top desk, the wisteria lamp in the corner with the tilted shade, the humid, oversweet odor of pipe tobacco and cologne permeating everything, the oriental rug faded where the afternoon sun burns through the tall windows . . . but here on the rug is another faded area, a large oval where someone has scrubbed it, where a stain has been lifted by hard work and whatever chemicals . . . .

He walked out. He tucked the gun in his pocket and looked around the room as though deciding what to do or what to take, glared at them as if to say, You think I came for your wallet, old man? You think I came for the fucking TV?

And walked out. She heard him in her brother's room, knocking pictures off the wall, toppling the dresser. Then in her room, hangers springing from the closet, drawers yanked open and clattering to the floor. He ran downstairs, and she heard him in the parlor, furniture crashing, glass breaking. She tried twisting her arms to loosen the tape, tried slipping a hand out, but couldn't. Her father lay next to her—if she could inch down, get to his wrists, she could chew the tape and free his hands. She rolled to her side, told her father what she was doing, expecting, hoping he would say Yes, hurry, but all he could say was Why?—Why was this happening to them?

Melody in her bathrobe, tugging her father through the snow in the backyard, over the fence and into the darkness of the neighbor's yard—she saw this in her mind, tip-toeing to her room for her bathrobe, the two of them hurrying down the service stairs to the rear door and out into the night . . . but the man returned before she could finish with the tape at her father's wrists; he walked in as she was lifting her head, a long strand in her mouth.

He did not hit her. He simply pulled her by the hair, back to where she'd been and then leaned over them, his breath quick and labored now, nearly a wheeze, and held the note where they both could read it, held it with a young and shaky hand, tapping it with the barrel of the gun. And her father said, "Dammit, there is no safe. Can't you hear? There is no safe." And the man shot him. In a clap of thunder she saw her father bounce once and then leak his life onto the rug through a ragged opening in his head. And the last thing she felt was the gun in her hair, and a roar, not a sound but a pressure, a rushing as of wind in a tunnel, a going away.

It is too much for her. With no warning she begins to retch. She hurries out the door and down the hall to the bathroom, reaches the toilet but can't throw up. She waits, but nothing happens. She considers pushing a finger down her throat, but can't do that either. This is how it has been since the hospital, this sense of choking, of something there but not there, something not in her throat but hidden in the damage at the base of her skull, poised as if to ambush her. And it will not come, it will not leave her.

She moves to the sink, and realizes—standing now at the mirror, seeing a face that is not her present face but a face from the future—that the dream was a sham, a hoax; that she was a fool to think she could walk in and walk out and rid herself of the past. She could almost laugh. She is both the joke and the joker, the dreamer and the dream itself. Oh, but the fear will come. She knows this now, she can see it in her eyes. It will leak from her slowly, drop by drop, year after year, as tears, as blood from a wound that will never heal.

She splashes water on her face, hoping to shrink the endlessness of it all. She must grow her hair back, she thinks, her wild hair that saved her, so that he thought he'd shot her in the center of the head when in fact the bullet had only creased her skull. She had turned to her father at that instant, turned her crown of curls that grew out past her shoulders and halfway down her back, and he'd shot her hair instead.

Hair that is gone now, barely long enough to cover the furrow in her head. She had been a month in the hospital, and then the long, slow recovery at her brother's in Omaha. The police had arrested the man that same night, in another house a block away—a drug addict, or a mental patient. She never did get it straight. She had come to in a haze of pain, the left side of her face sinking in a pool of blood—her and her father's, the sickening, fruity smell of it in her throat— and had pushed herself across the floor, then back with the telephone cord in her mouth until the old metal phone toppled from the desk. And later, out of the hospital and at her brother's house, the nightmares began: a man in a ski mask stalking her, catching her, the gun tangled in her hair. Every night she'd wake up screaming, and her brother, at first troubled, even frightened, and then later impatient, condescending, would tell her it was okay, everything was okay now, the man was in prison. As if that were enough.

Mel leaves the bathroom. She feels heavy; the gray light in the upstairs hall seems to press against her; the air settles in her lungs like ash. She forces herself past the bedrooms and down the stairs, and when she enters the living room Beth gets off the couch. The front door is still open, and now a chill is added to the gloomy silence of the house.

"There's nothing I want here," Mel says, and Beth blinks, looks around at the furniture, and then touches the arm of the couch.

"This is very old."

"Yes, it's stuffed with horsehair," Mel says, impatient now. "And that's marble on the tables, and the chairs are antiques. So is the rug."

"Worth a fortune," Beth says, almost dreamily.

"Then maybe you should sell it for a fortune."

Mel is about to add, And buy yourself a new hat . . . and can think of a dozen other phrases too cruel to be witty . . . but she is aware of an almost visible warmth from Beth, a concern that has nothing to do with the house.

Beth hesitates, and clears her throat. "Honey, all your books, all your clothes in your room. You don't want any of it?"

Suddenly Mel wants out. Out of the house, out of the city. She's had this idea about hitchhiking to Alaska, working construction or crewing a fishing boat, something hard and out of doors. Something far away.

"Are there papers to sign?"

Beth smiles. "Your brother took care of that. We're set to close in a month."

Mel lifts her knapsack by the strap, slings it over her shoulder. "Then can you give me a ride? To the freeway downtown?"

"Honey, of course." Beth starts toward her, but stops abruptly when Mel turns. From behind Mel she says, "But why don't we have lunch at Andre's first? Or there's this cute little place on the downtown mall."

Mel can't answer. The idea of lunch is so absurd she feels like crying. She steps outside onto the porch. The sun winks through the upper branches of the sycamore in a way that is familiar. When she was small, five or six, she carried a serving dish from the dining room and filled it with dirt from around the rhododendrons in the front yard. Her father spanked her, struck her for the first time. And then on the porch he picked her up, and in a rare show of affection, with the sun over his shoulder winking rainbows through her tears, he kissed her cheek and told her he was sorry.

Mel hands Beth the key, and Beth locks the front door. The fragmented light has a hypnotic effect, and as they walk to the car Mel sees too clearly what will happen to the old sycamore—she sees them cutting it, limb by limb, grinding the branches in one of those infernal machines, the dust swirling high into the summer sky.

Beth opens the car door for Mel and says, "Can't I take you to a friend's place? Or a hotel? Listen, Hon, I don't have to return to the office. You could come out to Cherry Hills. The last of my daughters is in college and my husband and I are all alone with too many empty rooms. It's such a lovely house, with a magnificent yard, with dogwood and cherry trees, and oh the flower garden, it's the perfect time of year.

You can stay, you know. We'd love to have you. It would be a nice place to relax."

"No thanks," Mel says, dropping herself on the front seat of Beth's car and shifting her knapsack to her lap, hugging it to her chest as a girl would hug a doll. Because she doesn't feel like relaxing. What she feels like is running. Running and running until she runs out of herself. What she feels like is disappearing, though she knows it wouldn't help. What she really feels like is killing someone.

Hardly Friends

Mel said, "Wake up, Hopalong. Here comes our ride."

Hank opened his eyes and saw the inside of his hat. Then he realized he had fallen asleep on the side of the highway. He sat up. The air smelled of wildflowers and boiling asphalt. He stood, unstuck himself from his sweaty shirt, and peered into the canyon.

It was a big Mercedes, silver, an older model, floating up the hill in the wrong lane, gobbling smoke and dust and potholes like a Hovercraft. It passed the long line of slow-moving trucks and dipped gracefully into the curve at the canyon wall, then powered out in a long arc, sun exploding off the windshield, heading directly for them now. Mel lifted her pack and slung a strap over her shoulder. She stuck out her arm, straight and high, thumb up. "Finally!" she said.

Mel was phenomenal. She could call a ride from a mile away. Not all the time, but enough that Hank wondered if she were psychic, although he didn't believe in such things. Five days they had been traveling together, up from Isla Mujeres and the Yucatan peninsula, through Veracruz, Mexico City, Guadalajara, and Mel had predicted most of the rides. She'd say, "See that smoky Ford third in line behind the bus?" Or, "The ten-wheel Dina with the red cab; not the first one, the one at the crest of the hill." Then she'd stick her thumb out and her chest out and maybe a hip, and sure enough, the bored Mexican in the badly leaning truck would pull off the road.

They had met on the ferry from the island to the Yucatan mainland. Hank sitting next to her and introducing himself, making the mistake of saying his friends called him Hopalong because he once wore spurs on his ski boots, said he was originally from Dallas, you see, but now he was a ski instructor and sometime bartender in Crested Butte, and every summer he hitchhiked south for his vacation— She cut him off. She said her name was Melody, but for Godsakes don't call her that, call her Mel. She didn't mention her last name. Or where she was from. For that matter, she didn't say much of anything, except that she was a writer, and sure, they could travel together, that would be good because she wouldn't have these damn macho Mexicans pawing at her all the time, but don't get the wild idea that traveling together meant sleeping together. So Hank didn't get the wild idea, although she wasn't unattractive and he found himself more than once wondering what she looked like beneath her baggy jeans and plain-wrapper shirts. Anyway, she was someone to talk at, if not with, and if she needed something to write about, well, here they were, Hopalong Hank and Melody Nobody, hardly friends but somehow companions, united by their foreignness and the unpredictable highways of Mexico. At least they had a common destination— Mazatlan on the Pacific coast, then across to La Paz and up the Baja to the States. And Mel could sure thumb a ride.

Now, above Guadalajara on Highway 15 at the northern rim of the *barrancas*—the canyons slicing through the Sierra Madre Occidental—Hank grabbed his knapsack and watched the Mercedes approach. Mel worked it hard—hip out, chest out, lots of volume on the mental channel—until the big sedan finally braked and stopped on the shoulder beyond. Mel marched up the road, small and confident. She took the front. Hank tossed the packs on the rear seat and followed them in.

The driver, a big gringo with a pocked face and wearing aviator's glasses, said nothing until they cleared the rim of the canyon and settled onto the long straightaway toward Tepic, the next city to the north. Then he announced his name. He was Joseph, or Joe, but everyone in Mexico called him the German. His car was Mister Wunderbar, didn't they think? He spoke English with a German accent. The car, he explained, was a rare 600S, "the most powerful, the most elegant sedan ever built," over twenty years old and in show-room condition. He smiled and fondled the gearshift, then smoothed a wisp of nonexistent hair on top of his shiny head. He wore a dark three-piece suit, a white shirt open at the collar, no tie. He looked forty, maybe forty-five, although the creases at the corners of his mouth and the loose folds beneath his chin said he was older, in his fifties. Hank eyed the suit, an odd piece of clothing, considering the heat. Mel said, "How did you get Mexican plates for this car?"

The German leaned into the wheel, turned the radio on and began searching for a station. Hank wondered about the plates also. With import taxes, the car would have cost a fortune in Mexico. And in Mexico it was illegal for a noncitizen to drive a car with Mexican tags, unless it was a rental vehicle, and this was no rental vehicle. The German sat back and adjusted his glasses. He looked at Mel.

"You are tourists," he said.

Mel narrowed her eyes. She hated being called a tourist. In Mexico City on the Zocalo, behind a group of picture-taking Americans wearing gaudy shirts and knee-length shorts, she told Hank she was a traveler, or a visitor, or a writer on assignment, but she was not and never would be a tourist!

To the German she said, "And you're a car thief."

The German laughed. He threw his head back and coughed, then gunned the engine and pulled out to pass a herd of smoking buses. Mr. Wunderbar rocketed down the left lane of the narrow highway with no chance of squeezing back in line. The German drove with his elbow out the window. The stink of diesel exhaust, mixed with the usual overripe scent of the Mexican countryside, blasted through the window and scoured the back of Hank's head. The German chuckled and shook his big face and chuckled again until he passed the lead bus and pulled in front. "I have been here eight years," he said, "and this is the first time I have seen a woman hitch-hiking." He glanced over at Mel. "This is not a good idea in Mexico, even if you are with your husband."

"He's not my husband," Mel said.

"Well then, your boyfriend."

"He's not my boyfriend either. We're traveling together . . . for convenience."

"Ah yes," the German said, "convenience." He lifted his chin and caught Hank's eye in the rearview mirror. He winked. "Well, it is convenient that I picked you up, is it not?" To Mel he said, "A great convenience. Because you are riding in the finest car in Mexico, with the finest driver in North America."

Mel rolled her eyes. She was about to respond when suddenly the German twisted the wheel and stood hard on the brake. Hank fell against the front seat, then reached for Mel who had slipped partway under the dash. The German cursed, but managed to swing the Mercedes around the huge diesel van sliding sideways across the highway, toward them. Behind it, a bony horse clopped from the road and into the trees. Mel sat up. The German cursed again, then shifted gears and pulled away from the van. "You see?" he said, almost shouting. "If not for Mr. Wunderbar we would have been killed! This is why you must travel first class in Mexico. It is the *campesinos*—the peasants—who cause the accidents. They do not understand speed as we do. They do not have the proper relationship with machinery!" Mel said nothing. She squinted as if to say, What the hell are you talking about?, but she said nothing. Hank almost voiced it himself. The near accident was obviously because of the horse, not the so-called peasant in the truck. And what was this nonsense about a relationship with machinery?

Nearing Tepic, the small terraced farms of the countryside gave way to gigantic fields tended by tractors, U.S. style. A crop duster catapulted skyward in front of the car, up and over the telephone wires next to the highway. Mel leaned forward and twisted her pixie head to watch it through the windshield, then quickly moved to the side window. The plane seemed to hang motionless above the wires, and then pivoted and dropped over the field, heading in the opposite direction. Mel followed it until she had nearly turned completely in her seat.

It was that way with Mel. The world was either "wow" or boring, the big movie or not worth her attention. The night before in Guadalajara she told Hank she was going to a whorehouse to see what it was like, and would he come along? A whorehouse?, he said. Was she crazy? He told her to go ahead, he'd wait for her in the park, watch her knapsack while she got herself killed. Eventually though, he caved in and accepted her offer to pay for the taxi, the drinks, whatever it took to get them through the experience. Mel bought pomade and a cheap hat at the bus station where they stored their packs in a locker. She greased her hair back and pulled the cap low on her forehead, and when she lifted the collar of her windbreaker, Hank had to admit she made a fairly convincing if not absurdly short guy. The taxi driver didn't flinch when she asked for the best house in the city. The bouncers at the door said nothing when she paid the cover charge. And the girls—Hank couldn't believe it, there must have been a hundred girls in that super-noisy, gymnasium-sized dance hall: gabbing in the bleachers, cruising the tables, dancing with each other on the basketball court. The girls thought Mel was cute, even sat on her lap, and claimed Hank was too big and too blond for them.

So this was Mel according to Hank: twenty-eight, twenty-nine years old, a writer because she couldn't help it, a traveler because she couldn't sit still, part adventurer, part desperate for a fresh idea. She loved the highway. She'd ride with anyone in anything, anywhere they'd take her except where she'd been. She'd eat, drink, and smoke what others wouldn't touch, and at night when she'd finally wind down, she'd choose the worst campsite possible, as bizarre a place as she could find, then speak of "auras" and "vibrations" and "telepathic conversations." And just when Hank would begin to wonder, she'd laugh and tell him it was all nonsense. After their twenty minutes in the brothel—all Hank could stand—she held his hand and kissed his cheek in the taxi back to the bus station, her tender moment. Then she scribbled for half the night in her journal.

The German said, "This is my home." They passed a Coca Cola factory on the right. Ahead on the left was a police car and a crowd of pedestrians near a wreck. The highway had become a wide city street, and the German settled behind the wheel, resigned to the traffic. "There are few *Norteamericanos* in Tepic," he said. "Which is why I like it. But there are times, you know, when it is good to be with your own kind." He laughed. "My wife tells me I will never become a Mexican, and she is right."

The German was married? Hank tried to picture his wife. A tall Nordic princess maybe? A stocky *frau* with a scarf?

At the traffic light in downtown Tepic the German took a cigarette from a case on the dash and lit it. "Please," he said, "I want you to visit my house for dinner. It is nearly *siesta*, and my wife will have something prepared." He looked at Mel. "Yes?"

Mel said, "Yes, why not." She turned and blinked her weimaraner eyes at Hank. Hank pondered his crusty jeans, the dead tennis shoes below. What he needed was a shower. But a home-cooked meal? Why not.

They passed motels and restaurants on the north end of town, and at a shady, manicured park, the German turned left onto a quiet street lined with giant eucalyptus trees. There were large two-story houses, some with elaborate iron-work fences fronting the sidewalk, and near the end of the block was a high whitewashed wall with bougainvillaea thick along the top. The German stopped at a wooden gate in the wall. He sounded the horn, and a moment later a shriveled man with a rake in his hand opened the doors. Two small girls in frilly white dresses ran from the house to the driveway. "Poppy," they shouted, jumping and flapping their tiny brown hands. "Poppy! Poppy!"

In the foyer they met Guadalupe, the German's wife. She was small and thin, barely out of her teens, Hank thought, with the dark, exaggerated features of a Mexican Indian. Her skin was the color of wet chamois, her eyes black and dreamy, and when she shook Hank's hand, she bowed, glancing shyly at his face. The old man from the gate appeared. The German bellowed orders, and quickly the man took the knapsacks upstairs to the second floor. A stocky woman dressed as a maid but who could easily have been Guadalupe's mother stood in a doorway, holding a baby.

They showered. Guadalupe brought clean clothes—one of her sundresses for Mel, a *guayabera* shirt and white slacks that were too tight for Hank. The maid took their dirty clothes, knapsacks and all, and disappeared downstairs. The problem, at least for Hank, was that there was only one bedroom, with the bathroom attached. Apparently Guadalupe thought the same as the German—that he and Mel were married, or close to married, or maybe that all Americans were above embarrassment—but perhaps there were no other bedrooms available. Anyway, Mel didn't seem to care.

She stripped in front of Hank and marched to the shower. He wasn't sure what astonished him the most, how quickly and easily she shed her clothes or how different her body was from what he had thought: no teddy bear figure there, no unwanted bulges hidden by loose clothing—only the curves of a strong and healthy woman.

Dinner was huachinango al mojo de ajo—red snapper in garlic butter—as delicious as Hank had ever tasted. The German made a point of announcing that Guadalupe had prepared it, not the maid. Three bites into his fish he stopped and took her by the wrist and forced her to stand, turned her and stroked her long black hair and made clucking noises to Hank, displaying her as if she were another exotic car in his collection. She blushed and sat down, and blushed again, and Hank had to look away: He couldn't decide if he was more embarrassed for her or for himself, as a guest of the German. She picked at her food while the German complained about Mexican politics—the Partido Revolucionario Institucional and ex-president Salinas, the guerrilleros in Oaxaca, corruption in the Policia Judicial Federal—after which and in nearly the same breath he proclaimed his love for Mexico. Take Mexican highways for instance; of course they were dangerous but that was the point. The highway in Mexico was still the frontier, the old west, and down here, he, the German, was the fastest gun— who could stop him? There wasn't a patrol car in the country could catch Mr. Wunderbar! . . . while Guadalupe, not understanding English and probably thankful she couldn't, kept bowls and cups and other objects moving smoothly around the table, until finally she excused herself and left the room with an armful of plates. Hank watched her go, half listening to the German rave about his fabulous car, half wishing Guadalupe would drop something so he could rush to the kitchen and help.

Mel drank brandy for dessert. The German finished his spiel on Mexican highways and began boasting about his house. Did they realize the furniture was imported from Spain? And the marble for the stairway—from Italy. "Look here," he said with a sweep of the hand, "all the glass in the front windows, made in the U.S.A.—bulletproof, you know." Mel gulped brandy. The German went on about the tile in the bathroom, the wood for the rear deck, the stones in the driveway. Finally Mel interrupted.

"How do you afford all this?" she said. "I mean, what is it that you *do*?"

Mel the reporter, Mel going for the jugular, Hank thought. But the German smiled, cool.

"I make deals," he said. "I buy and sell things." He smoothed an eyebrow. "Commodities."

"What?" Mel said, "Coffee? Beans?"

The German folded his napkin and placed it on the table. He stared at Mel for a second, then called to Guadalupe for more brandy. He turned to Hank.

"Please, I want you to be my guests for the night. In the

morning I must continue north. If you wish to come along, you are welcome."

"Where north?" Hank said.

"Across the mountains to Durango, then to Chihuahua and the border." He looked at Mel. "Perhaps you will see firsthand what it is that I do, as you put it."

Guadalupe brought another bottle of brandy from the kitchen. The twins ran in behind her. They smiled at Mel, and when Mel smiled back, they both spoke to her in squeaky Spanish, one on each side of her chair.

Hank said, "That's a generous offer." Mel shot him a look. He said, "But I think we'll continue up the coast, take the ferry to Baja."

"Of course," the German said. He poured another round. Mel lifted one of the twins to her lap, and immediately had to lift the other who had begun to cry. The German spoke to Guadalupe in Spanish, then turned to Mel. "I must rest. My wife will show you the property. There is a pool if you care to use it, a tennis court also." He stood up abruptly, smiled at no one in particular, and walked out. Guadalupe blushed.

Mel slept all afternoon. Hank tried the liver-shaped pool with the Spanish tile, but found it too small to swim laps in. He served aces to no one on the tennis court, then walked to the opposite end and served them back. He practiced Spanish on the maid in the kitchen and found out she was Guadalupe's mother, and then he walked to the plaza in downtown Tepic where he met a pretty Mexican girl and her two giggling sisters who needed a chaperon to a bar. When he returned to the house it was nearly midnight, and everyone but Mel had gone to bed. He found her on a chair in the bedroom, writing in her journal.

"You're drunk," she said, without looking up.

There was one double bed in the room. Hank sat on it.

Mel said, "At least you're not hung over."

The sandals Guadalupe had loaned him cut into his ankles. He undid the straps. "Is that why you're up?" he said. "Too sick to lie down?"

She shrugged. She smiled a tiny smile, a mouse grin, then pulled a limp washrag from the back of her neck and dropped it on the floor. And then she did a strange thing: She closed her journal and came to him. She took off his sandals. She lifted his tired feet to the bed, then pushed him back gently and arranged the pillow under his head. She massaged his shoulders, his arms, lifted his shirt and slid her hands across his chest.

She sat up. She chewed her lip, then said, "What do you think he is?"

"What? Who, the German?"

She said, "You know what I think? I think he's a spy."

So much for the massage, Hank thought. Or what might have followed. He said, "A spy? No . . . more like a drug smuggler. Or maybe you're right. Maybe he's CIA, which would make him a drug smuggler *and* a spy."

"No, I'm serious. I snuck into the den. The walls are covered with maps. And all the cabinets and desk drawers were locked."

"Maps? How's that make him a spy?"

"I don't know, but why would someone into commodities have a war room in his house? There's this huge map of Mexico on one wall, with different colored pins stuck on various cities. I'll bet those are his assignments. You know, he lives here and travels all over Mexico doing his thing. Or maybe he's an assassin—he disappears someone in Mexico City or Guadalajara, then comes home to his cozy house and his innocent wife and no one is the wiser."

You must be joking, Hank wanted to say. But she wasn't, so he didn't. Better to play this out, he thought, throw in a non sequitur of his own.

"I'd say he's your basic garden-variety coke smuggler, probably has fifty kilos in Mr. Wunderbar's trunk. He picks up a load in Guadalajara, stops at his house for the night, then does his 'Thunder Road' thing to the border the next day."

Mel said, "But why would he invite us along?"

"Why not? The police stop him, he's out of the profile— three people in the car, two with tourist cards, one a woman."

Mel thought for a minute. She had this habit of chewing her lip. "No . . . he's not sleazy enough for dope. No diamond-crusted Rolex, no rings or chains. And that suit— you ever see a dope dealer dress like that?"

She grabbed her journal. She found her pen and walked to the chair, then sat and began to write. Hank loosened his belt and pushed himself back against the headboard where he could watch her. She sat with her knees together and feet apart, hunched over the journal in her lap. Her hand floated across the page, jumped back, and floated across again. The rest of her was eerily still; she seemed not even to breathe, as though by the motion of her hand she had hypnotized herself. Hank felt heavy. He felt himself sinking into the bed. Finally, Mel came up for air and looked at him, or through him.

"Remember the rides I called?" She tapped her chin with the pen. "Educated guesses, really—a certain car at the right time, the driver alone. But not the Mercedes. I knew that car would stop. I was sure, even before it reached the bottom of the canyon." She paused, and said, "He has the strangest aura I've ever seen. Very close to his body and dark red, like an autumn sunset."

Hank said, "What?"

"Not like yours. Yours is soft and airy and full of light—I could get lost in your aura." She bit the pen. "Something is going to happen to the German. Something important. And I have the weird feeling that I'm involved, as though there's a connection between us . . . like I'm compelled to find out who he is and what he does . . . as if he were a character in a story I'm about to write." She looked up. "Does that make sense?"

"None whatsoever," Hank said, although a little too

quickly: It made sense because it was classic Mel, Mel grasping at psychic straws, Mel searching for the next roller coaster. A spy? A smuggler? The German was probably what he said he was, a bean salesman. Just another gringo who couldn't make it at home, so he comes to Mexico and buys his dream car and his child wife and whatever it takes to convince himself he's got it made. Not a bad guy, really. Lonely because he's a jerk. Generous to strangers . . . of his "own kind." Clean sheets on the bed . . . .

Mel moved to the desk. She sat with her back to the room, a Tensor lamp pulled low over her journal.

Hank woke to the sound of small animals galloping through his head. Then he heard the twins shouting in the hall.

No Mel.

The bed was still made. He was still dressed in the *guayabera* shirt and white pants. But it was definitely morning, late morning if he read the window light correctly. He fumbled for his watch. And then he saw the note, a sheet torn from her journal.

He caught the one o'clock bus. He didn't even think about hitchhiking—he walked straight to the bus station and bought a ticket for Mazatlan. The twins made a big deal of waving good-bye in the front yard, Guadalupe fixed a breakfast he couldn't eat, and her mother the maid brought his clothes and his knapsack to the bedroom, ironed and folded. This, in reverse order, was his morning. Now, on the giant, double-decker *Tres Estrellas de Oro* express, humming across the lowlands two hours north of Tepic, he dug out the note and read it again:

Hopalong—

I've decided you were right—the German is into dope. But I'm not sure how. Not a smuggler. More like a mid-level boss, arranging shipments, payoffs, that sort of thing. Well, anyway, I guess I'll find out soon enough, won't I? Wish me luck.

Love,

Mel

And that was all. No address, no phone number, no way to find her. Yesterday in Guadalajara she said she'd surprise him someday and show up in Crested Butte for a ski lesson—some winter day, there she'd be, plowing the bunny hill and making a fool of herself, just for him—wouldn't that be a shocker? Sure, he told her, shock him out of his socks. "Yeah," he said now, "a real shocker," and then realized where he was—on the bus, talking to the window, out loud.

The woman next to him, the fat woman in the muu muu, said, "Pardon?"

Hank said it was nothing, just thinking.

He was surrounded by Americans, some kind of tour. When he boarded the bus in Tepic Muu Muu and her friends had accosted him with questions—where was he from, where was he going, was he traveling alone in Mexico?—on and on. Finally they ignored him when he said he was tired. Now, however, Muu Muu seemed delighted that he had broken the silence. She leaned forward and eyed his knapsack on the floor between them. "You actually camp out in this backward country?" she said.

Hank said he did. Mazatlan, he thought; another two hours he'd be in Mazatlan. From there he could take a flight to the states.

Muu Muu said, "I don't know how. It was all I could do to stay at the Holiday Inn in Guadalajara. Do you know it took three hours for room service? I asked for a ham sandwich and they brought soap. Can you believe it?"

Hank said he could.

"Then Aeromexico loses our reservations, so we have to take a bus to Mazatlan. I said to my sister Irene—that's her over there with the pink sunglasses—I said, No way Jose, I'm not riding on a Mexican bus, not with all the horrible accidents you hear about."

Just then the bus slowed and came to a stop. It started forward again, then stopped. They were on open highway, but barely moving at the end of a long line of traffic. Eventually they reached the site of the accident. Hank saw the truck first, overturned and spilled partway across the highway. He stood up. His stomach sank. He was sure there was another vehicle involved, and for some reason, equally sure it was the big Mercedes. And then he saw the car, or what was left of it, down the embankment and partially hidden in the bushes. It was yellow. It was a taxi, an old yellow taxi.

Muu Muu said, "See what I mean? You can't go fifty feet, there's a wreck! '*Mañana*' they say. 'Come south and relax, enjoy the slow pace of Mexico.' Bunch of speeding maniacs, if you ask me."

The bus wound through the gears, clear of the accident now and gaining speed. Hank excused himself and stepped into the aisle. He felt nauseated. He locked himself in the bathroom, then couldn't throw up. Why had he been certain he would see the remains of the Mercedes? Damn it, why did Mel go with the German! And damn it, why did it matter if she did? Who was she anyway? God knew, she wasn't his type. Wired, blunt, eyes that saw through you, too damn short—growing up in Dallas he'd been a jock since grade school, the big football star. It seemed like every month there had been a new cheerleader or majorette calling the house, right through college until he dropped out and became a ski bum. Even then there were plenty of women, tall and classy, weekend lovers mostly, but some offering more. Hank was too young to remember his father before he died, and maybe it was because of his big sister and his mother, both tall and beautiful and nearly smothering him with their protective love, that he never found one girl, that there were so many girls—and now here he was chasing Mel, Mel the mysterious, the unavailable—Mel who was gone.

He turned the handle, but the door wouldn't open. He

twisted the lock, first one way, then all the way back until he heard it snap. Wonderful. He was trapped in the tiny, stinking bathroom. He leaned on the wall and held his headache, knowing it would soon worsen—in a minute he'd have to kick the door out, then deal with the codriver or the driver or whoever else wanted to argue. Why was he on the damn bus anyway? He hated buses. He hated all forms of public transportation, which is exactly the reason he chose to hitchhike through Mexico—to be free of the packaged tours, the commercial traps, the whining tourists. But then he wondered if there was really any difference between Muu Muu and himself. Hitchhiking or riding the bus, they were both on the highway and the highway wasn't Mexico; Mexico was ten feet on either side, going nowhere, saying nothing, ignoring the madmen rushing by.

The bus slowed. Another wreck, Hank thought. He pushed against the door, leaned back, then hit it with his shoulder. It popped open, quietly, and he started up the aisle. They were entering a small town, a village no more than a hundred yards long—one ancient pink church, forty or fifty adobe houses, an open-front, tin-roofed restaurant at the side of the road. But there were *topes*—concrete speed-bumps across the highway—and the bus had to slow to a near stop. Hank passed Muu Muu and kept going until he reached the front. There, parked to one side in a gas station, with the hood up and with a mob of grubby children leaning on the fender, was the big silver Mercedes.

There was no sign of the German, not at the pumps, not in the garage. No sign of Mel either. Hank turned and hurried down the aisle. Muu Muu stared wide-eyed as he yanked his knapsack off the floor. By the time he returned to the front, the bus had cleared the last of the *topes* and was accelerating past the north end of town. And then he saw her, on the shoulder near a crossroad, standing with her knapsack at her feet—no thumb in the air, no hip out, just standing there watching the traffic. Hank told the driver to pull over.

"Hopalong!" Mel said as he stepped down. "I knew it was you!"

The door closed with a hiss. The bus sighed, then began its roll onto the highway, loud as an airplane. Hank waited until it rounded a curve, then asked about the German.

She shrugged. "He's on his way home."

Hank said he saw the car at the gas station. With the hood up.

Mel grinned, an imp. She dug in her bag and came up with a distributor cap. "Of course it's at the gas station! The German went to the men's room and I went to the women's room and somebody went under the hood—except I didn't go to the women's room. He thinks some kids stole it. It's weird because half the people there saw me do it, but no one said a thing. You know what that bastard did? We're not ten miles out of Tepic, he starts hitting on me, telling me his wife's a bad lay, crap like that. Pretty soon he's offering me money, like I'm a whore or something. And then it gets so bad he's grabbing himself and sweating, getting real pushy and beginning to scare me, until finally we get to the gas station and he runs in the men's room. Terrific, I'm saying to myself, the character in my story turns out to be a weirdo twice my size who's not about to let me go. But I know he loves his car more than his women. So when he comes out and discovers what's wrong with Mr. Wunderbar, he's too upset to breathe. Finally he calms down and tells me he's got extra parts in the trunk, but no distributor cap—that's at home in his garage along with every other nut and bolt Mercedes ever made. He says to me, 'Watch the car. I'll be back before dark!' That was, oh, I guess an hour and a half ago." She squinted at the afternoon sun, then up at Hank. "I knew you'd come along eventually, so I waited."

Hank said, "The German went home?"

Mel nodded. She smiled.

He said, "How did he manage that without a car?"

Mel made a face. "That idiot. You know what he did? There's a bus through here every ten minutes, at least. First class, second class, whatever—they all stop if you flag them down. But no, he can't take a bus, not him, buses are too dangerous, and anyway, they're driven by peasants who don't relate to machinery. So what does he do? It takes him twenty minutes, but finally he locates the only one in town. A taxi. He rents an old dilapidated taxi, insists on driving it himself. Puts the driver in the backseat. Can you believe it?"

Hank said he could.

Old Max

There is the wall, and then jagged hills all around, and above the wall and the hills, the clean white dome of sky, so clean you can almost feel it, smooth beyond measure, silky hot. Where the dome meets the horizon it is all snaggle-toothed hills, so that everything above resembles the inside of an egg, broken in half, and if you roll your head back and gaze toward the sun, straight straight up, squinting, sweat burning your eyes, you can feel yourself float, rise on a wave of heat and then soar above the wall and the hills, higher and higher.

Alex, leaning on his shovel and with his face to the sky, feels his neck pop, and at that very instant hears Crummage, that pig, shouting from the far side of the field. "Pitts, you dummy!"—on and on while Alex pulls his handkerchief from his pocket and wipes his face, wipes the sweat and—if he didn't know better, if this had been another life—wipes what could have been tears from his cheeks. He opens his eyes and sees what he always sees.

What they did, years ago, they had convicts build the wall, cut the stone from the hill behind the prison, brick by brick; what used to be a rocky bluff covered with sage and pine is now a vertical scar three hundred feet high, the entire side of it down to the fences nearby. The rest is in the wall—thirty feet tall and half a mile long, thick enough to walk on.

"You gettin' a tan, Pitts? You on the beach?" Crummage has crossed the ditch and come up behind Alex, laughing even though nothing is funny. "Get your ass in gear, boy."

This ditch is part of a new irrigation project for the town. The old sluice has run west to east through the prison compound for years. Now they want a spillway to the south, past the clinic and death row, under the wall and through the park out front. There are six inmates to dig it with picks and shovels, ten hours a day, seven days a week, another hundred yards before they bring in the cement trucks. Alex knows he is on the crew for a reason—he is big and strong and they figure he is dumb enough to do what he's told.

"If you're sick, Pitts, get a pass from the clinic." Crummage, smiling broadly, throws out a hand in the direction of the buildings a football field away.

Alex has this choice. He can drop his shovel and head for the clinic—men have keeled over in this heat, and there are always lawsuits pending against the state . . . but a trip to the clinic means two days' lay-in, no gym or yard privileges, too many questions from a suspicious nurse who couldn't give a damn if you lived or died. Alex has this choice, and one other—he can swing the shovel, turn his back to Crummage and do his job, dig for his lousy meals and what little freedom he can eke out of a day.

"Pitts, you got a problem?"

Alex looks up at him. Crummage is day-shift labor foreman, pushing sixty and close to retirement. He is as thick and wrinkled as a tree stump, and where his eyes should be there are tiny holes covered by cheap, wire-rimmed sunglasses he never removes. His mouth is loose, mocking.

"Because if you do, Pitts, we can take care of it. Just you and me, son."

He steps in front of Alex, hands still on his hips, now with his chin up, close. Alex can smell his breath. The old man's brow is dry, not a drop of sweat, and Alex hates him for this; he could kill this man with one punch, bust his overripe head before the guard in the tower could shoot. Crummage is unarmed. He is fat and sloppy, and Alex has seen a thousand like him, Alex growing up in state homes and detention centers, hating the guards with a fire in his chest he could barely control, hating them the way he hated his father who beat him with fists when he was a child, punished him for crying, and later, when the tears dried forever, punished him for talking, for saying I'm sorry, for saying anything at all, until Alex quit that also—and all the while he wanted to kill the man, silently, never saying a word—just kill him and walk away.

Crummage must sense this because he drops his hands

and shakes his head. Alex knows what Crummage thinks—
that a man who cannot talk is stupid; that a man who is
silent is blind and deaf as well. But Crummage knows that
Alex can feel. He knows because he taunts Alex, because he
pushes him to the edge and then a little beyond, almost
enough, before he backs off and shakes his head.

Alex stabs at the side of the ditch, gets a foot on the shovel
and buries it to the handle. The dirt is sandy in places, wet
and heavy in others. There are rocks, chunks of shale by the
thousands, and the digging is uneven, fitful. The sun
scorches the back of his neck, boils the sweat on his shirt.
Yesterday he felt his knees give out, and today it is his feet—
an ache he can't quite place, all over in his thick, state-issue
brogans. But his back and shoulders are strong, and he can
count on his arms; his arms will be the last to go.

What they did, a hundred years ago they bought this land
in a two-horse town and built a prison on it. It is an old-style
penitentiary, with multitiered, Alcatraz-like cellhouses surrounded by massive stone walls, the walls dominated by six
stone towers topped with old, dishpan searchlights. The cellhouses and support buildings have been renovated numerous
times, and recently when the Feds sued, they built a modern
medical unit just inside the south wall. Now all the real convicts are gone. Now there are new prisons scattered far out on
the plains: low-slung affairs with high-tech fences, prefabs
and modulars resembling bunkers by day and spacecraft at
night. They are filled with youngsters, gangs of kids with crazy

hairdos and city faces, mouths full of chatter that Alex cannot listen to. And now Old Max is reserved for the ill and the aged, the cripples, men who can no longer care for themselves. Some so old they do not belong in prison.

But there are a few left over from the days when Old Max was the only prison in the state, cons they keep around to do the heavy work—Alex and Lincoln, Gomez and Lafayette, Stansky and Peters—the inside labor gang. Peters is a little guy, slender but tough. Everywhere he has been he has screwed up, all the other facilities, and now they are either offering him a final chance or have put him here as a way of getting rid of him. Peters' gaunt, pocked face is dominated by large doe-like eyes you try not to look at, and part of his nose is missing, a crude notch gouged out of his nostril, which lends him a damaged, lopsided look, worse than if he had lazy eye. Alex tolerates him, but Peters fancies himself a con man; he is sly and quick, and Alex is wary of him.

Now Crummage has crossed back to the other side of the ditch, and Alex watches as he approaches Peters. The others are there, Oscar Lincoln, Gomez and Lafayette, Big Stansky, but Crummage is a comedian and he picks his straight men carefully—Alex because he can't talk, and Peters because he is six inches shorter and half Crummage's weight.

"Peters, when all this is done, what say you and me go fishin'?" Crummage grins and winks at no one in particular. "Right here in this ditch you dug, bet there'll be some nice trout." He hooks his thumbs in his belt and stands in front of Peters who is partway in the ditch. Crummage is neckless; his jaw juts forward and his head slopes upward to a point, as though all that really mattered in his skull had grown dense and had settled to the bottom, where his mouth is. "You like trout, Peters? I'll bet you do." He guffaws. His pendulous belly hangs over the ditch directly above Peters who continues to dig with his shovel. Crummage twists his head to the right. "Hey Gomez, what do they call trout in Spanish? *Trucha*, right? Yeah, *trucha*." He turns back to Peters. "Maybe you and me, Peters, we could have some *trucha* one of these nights. Or put it this way—*you* could have the *trucha*, and me, I'll supply it." He laughs loudly, then wheezes. "Peters, you a little old for me, but you ain't bad. 'Specially when you bend over like that."

It happens fast, almost too fast for Alex to see. The shovel falls away from Peters' hand and immediately he is up under Crummage's gut—just there, attached to Crummage, lips tight and eyes like coal, arm and shoulder and entire upper body pushing into Crummage's abdomen. Suddenly Crummage wheels around and stumbles, picks himself up and stumbles again. His glasses hang from one ear, and his tiny eyes are now huge and amazed. He is running, holding his stomach and bellowing, and Alex sees the guard emerge from the tower with a rifle. Peters, dull gray shank in his hand, the end of it shiny with Crummage's blood, casually sits down on the bank of the ditch, drops the knife in the dirt, and kicks it aside.

Security arrives—more than twenty blueshirts round the

corner of the nearest cellhouse and sprint for the field. Crummage has collapsed fifty yards from the ditch, and the guard in the tower is shouting for Alex and the others to drop their picks and shovels and keep their hands where he can see them; Peters sits elbows on knees, head lowered, perfectly still. They'll kill him, Alex thinks—he'll spend a lifetime in the hole where they'll slowly kill him. This is how it is. This is how it will always be.

There is a trace of blue in the afternoon sky, but mostly it is white hot, the sun baking the air to a ceramic hardness. Alex tilts his head back until his face is nearly horizontal with the ground. He can relax this way, block it all out, float for a minute in an eerie balance, squinting through the moisture in his eyes. And then it occurs to him that there are no cracks in this dome, that nothing lives in this sky, that birds could never fly here.

Wildflowers

Toni leaned forward from the back of the open Jeep and handed my mother a pair of plastic goggles. "Ma," she said, "wear these. They'll keep the dust out of your eyes."

My poor mother. Toni had zipped her into my wool jacket and wrapped her legs in the picnic blanket, but had forgotten to bring a scarf. Now, in the wind, my mother's gray hair stood from the top of her head like a wire broom. Toni shouted in her ear, "Ma, you look like Don King!"

My mother couldn't possibly know who Don King is, I thought, and anyway, she was too preoccupied to care, gripping the seat with both hands, staring wide-eyed behind her goggles. This was her first ride in a Jeep. This was also the first time she had been west of Pittsburgh, and yesterday when she arrived she found herself wheezing in the thin Rocky Mountain air. Now, riding shotgun in my ancient, topless Jeep, she had all the air she could stand. She gulped and turned to me. "Jarrold, is the King Ranch around here? Isn't that in Texas?"

We passed the entrance to the ski area. Toni pointed out the green slopes, the empty lifts, the construction site that would eventually be my restaurant. This restaurant, my attempt at a new way of life, or at least a new way to make a living, would be open, I hoped, before the first heavy snow of the coming winter. My mother took a long look at the skeletal frame of two-by-fours, then nodded. I knew that subtle dip of her head. It was her way of saying "Yes . . . the restaurant." Her way of disapproving while trying not to disappoint me. Two winters ago I came out here for a ski vacation, and last year when my wife divorced me and left for Florida, I sold my share of Penn Chemical and moved to this sleepy Colorado town for good. Now I owned a two-story Victorian on a quiet street behind the church, next door to a rustic cabin full of an energetic blonde—my neighbor Toni, avid skier, accomplished mountaineer, and the first woman to hang glide off Mount Crested Butte. Her last name is Flowers, and at the moment this vigorous and sometimes loquacious Ms. Flowers was explaining to my mother how she had convinced me to hire her as future manager, maitre d', menu artist, waitress, and hat-check girl of my new restaurant on the hill.

My mother, her round, begoggled face plowing a stiff wind, said nothing in return. Toni smiled weakly, then leaned across and tightened my mother's seat belt. We had reached the end of the paved highway and were now on the dirt road that would take us high into the Elk Mountains, past the ghost town of Gothic, up to Emerald Lake and on to Schofield Pass at timberline. Beyond Schofield, the road becomes a steep, rocky path, a narrow ledge on a cliff descending into the Crystal River Valley and the town of Marble. From there it is an easy ride over McClure Pass and around to Kebler, then back to our town of Crested Butte. This one-day adventure, this short but spectacular circle through Colorado mountain country, was Toni's idea. A week ago when I sent the plane ticket to Philadelphia I told Toni I had no idea how I would entertain my mother— Crested Butte is an outdoor town and my mother is an indoor person. "It's simple," Toni said. "Show her what she's been missing. Take her where flatlanders never go."

I drove slowly. We passed meadows popping with wild-flowers, thick, feathery stands of aspen, dark tunnels of spruce on our ascent. Near Gothic, my mother appeared to relax a little, but she still held on tight, stealing quick glances at the forest whenever she felt it safe to take her eyes from the road. We mounted a series of narrow switchbacks, the Jeep lurching over boulders half its size, my mother's head lolling forward, then springing back as the wheels caught. I hoped she wouldn't be sick. This was too much for her, I thought. How could I have brought my plump, seden-tary, seventy-five-year-old mother into this rugged terrain inhabited by pumas and mountain goats and their foolish human counterparts? Why hadn't I stoked the fire in the fire-place and brought her a weekend's stack of books to read?

Why had I listened to the chatty advice of the adventurous Toni Flowers?

But at Emerald Lake, a glassy pond with postcard views high on a saddle in the Elk Mountains, a strange thing happened. We had spread the blanket on the stones at the shoreline, next to a flat rock that served as our picnic table. My mother nibbled at her sandwich, and to my surprise, she rather quickly downed a glass of red wine that Toni had put in her hand. My mother is not a drinker. She will sip partway through an occasional Manhattan at a restaurant or a party, but this, I have always thought, was in deference to my father, so as not to embarrass him in front of his hard-drinking country club friends and their wives. At sea level, a glass of wine, or even a Manhattan, may have little effect. But at eleven thousand feet, a thimble-full of alcohol can do astonishing things to the head. Toni had taken my mother's camera and hiked to a point a hundred yards up the mountain, and my mother, now working on her second glass, had perched herself on a log at the edge of the lake. I saw that she was rocking ever so slightly, and when she looked up to watch a hawk skid past a snowy ridge, she leaned far to the left, as if she too might drop and soar to the limitless sky in the valley below.

She sighed when I approached. "Oh Jarrold, this *really* is *beautiful* country," she said. She seemed to float above the log. "I had no *idea!*"

This was not my mother talking. She is a private person

who is frequently thought of as shy, a woman who rarely offers an opinion or exhibits her feelings. I have never known her to swoon.

"I *like* Toni," she said. "I like the way she calls me *Ma*." She smiled. If a smile can be a wink, then I had just seen my mother wink.

"Toni's a friend," I said. "She's helping me with the restaurant."

I studied my mother's face, the waves of freckles that had widened and merged with age, the once-blue eyes that were gray now, like her hair, and yet alert, still quick to shine. I felt compelled to change the subject, but I couldn't think of a suitable topic. I have been in this predicament before with my parents—there are times when they seem strangers to me, or I to them. I groped for a question, then came up with the one I had intended not to ask.

"How's Dad?" I said.

My mother shooed an invisible fly with her hand. "Oh, you know. The same. He still thinks you threw your life away. He can't understand why the vice president of Penn Chemical became a cook in the wilderness."

Ah, yes—the restaurant, the spike I had driven through my father's expectations. Half my life I was number two behind number one at Penn Chemical. Number one is R. Harold Wells, my father. When I resigned last year, when I told him it wasn't worth the ulcers and the insomnia and the monthly liquor bills, he stomped from my office and refused my calls.

I've spoken to him since, two or three times by phone, but I am careful not to mention my departure, or my new life in Colorado.

My mother stood and brushed herself off and looked down at the log. "Good log," she said, as if praising a family pet. And then she smiled that same smile at me. "I'll take care of your father," she said. "You take care of that lovely restaurant."

Lovely two-by-fours? She's bombed, I thought. But her eyes were sharp, as crisp as the thin mountain air. Could she have applauded my move? I wondered. Had she disagreed with the infallible Harry Wells?

My mother poured out the rest of the wine, then passed her hand and the empty glass in a swooping motion, encompassing sky and mountain and lake and sky. "This is an *extraordinary* place," she said. "Absolutely *phenomenal!*"

Toni returned, and while I packed the picnic gear into the Jeep, she and my mother walked south along the rocky shore. From a distance they looked like schoolgirls, Toni with her arm around my mother's shoulder, her long blonde ponytail swinging behind her blue parka. My mother watched as Toni skipped stones to the middle of the lake, and then they started back, stopping to examine something in the rocks, pointing at the mountain, waving at me, and laughing. I watched them for a long time. Toni, when you first meet her, is the sort of person who either charges past you or forever runs in your shoes; she either loves you or fiercely ignores you. She is like the Rocky Mountains—there are no rounded corners to Toni; she is a land of sharp choices. Yesterday when I invited her to the airport to greet my mother I wasn't sure how the meeting would go. I think my mother panicked when Toni, whom she had never met, nor even heard of before, grabbed her and kissed her and practically carried her to the parking lot, "Ma" this and "Ma" that. All the way home my mother sat quietly in the front seat of Toni's car, politely nodding, slightly bug-eyed and out of breath, wondering, I thought, where I had found this blonde stick of dynamite and what we both should do about it. At the house, my mother said she wasn't feeling well. Toni left, telling us to be ready early for our Jeep trip. My mother wandered from room to room and then finally retired for the night, lost, it seemed, disoriented in this airless, alien world I had brought her to.

Now, at Emerald Lake, my mother had apparently made a remarkable recovery. She seemed bursting with vigor, matching strides with Toni as they approached. I could hear them giggling, looking at me, and then giggling again, and at one point my mother must have revealed an old secret from my past because Toni nearly doubled over laughing, pointing at me and saying "Him? Really?" Women have a delightful way of conspiring, of discovering a common thread and pooling their energy; together they are capable of creating out of nothing a rather sudden and substantial something. Even women as oddly different as Elizabeth

Wells and Toni Flowers. Here they were, I thought, near the top of the world, two women at opposite poles of character and age, smirking at me from the outer reaches of my understanding. Here was my mother who was not my mother, high on wine and lack of oxygen, cavorting with my neighbor Toni who, dipping her head to savor a whisper, was beaming at me, sending a message I hadn't seen before. How did this happen? What bizarre recipe had the cosmos followed to cook this? What part mountain air, I thought, how much tipsy mother, how many tablespoons of spicy blonde?

In the Jeep, my mother slapped her goggles on and told me she was ready. Toni said nothing, but I could feel her eyes on the back of my head. I have known Toni for six months. We are neighbors, not lovers. She is a handsome woman, which is to say she is beautiful in a natural and athletic way; she wears no makeup, and I have never seen her in a dress. But that does not make her less desirable, not to me or to the squads of younger men in town who try to date her. She is in her thirties and I am in my fifties, and I have often thought this age difference to be a barrier, to her at least. But I have also, many times I must admit, wondered what she would look like in a dress, or less. And now, as we headed into the high, flat meadows of Schofield Pass, I had that same exquisite picture of her in my mind—the athletic Toni Flowers, striding toward me across this very meadow, sheltered by her long hair and little else. I pulled the Jeep to the side of the road and took off my jacket.

My mother grinned, unbuckled herself, and got out. "Wildflowers," she said, scanning a field of bright yellow rydbergii. She and Toni walked off to pick flowers while I drove to the northern end of the Schofield tundra to check the stream we would have to ford. It was high, but I knew we'd make it, and when I returned, my mother was sitting by the road, sniffing a bouquet of fairy primrose and alpine forget-me-nots. Her face glowed in the intense sunlight. In her tan slacks and my tartan jacket she seemed remarkably adapted to the harsh environment, like a short, thick bush. She stood, took Toni's hand, and walked to the Jeep.

"Why doesn't anyone *live* up here?" she said as she buckled herself in. "And where's this Son-of-a-Bitch Gulch?"

I looked at Toni. Toni shrugged.

I answered the first question. I told my mother what I knew about Schofield, the mining camp that briefly flourished before the turn of the century, the horrible conditions in winter, the enormous problems they had getting supplies through the snow. I said it was too far, too high, too remote. As to the waterfall in the nearby and aptly named gulch, I wished Toni hadn't mentioned it—I pictured my mother struggling on that rugged path, perhaps twisting an ankle, or worse.

Toni said, "Ma, maybe we'll hike to the waterfall next time. We better continue so we can get home before dark."

My mother took this excuse for what it was, I knew, but she smiled and patted Toni's arm as if to say, Good going, you read his thoughts. And then she turned and gazed toward the field. "His father will never see this," she said, referring, in the same breath, to the sea of wildflowers and, odd as it seemed at the moment, to R. Harold Wells. "He's afraid of the great outdoors. His idea of wilderness is a sand trap on a golf course." She seemed gay to the point of being flip. She stuck her hands on her hips and scanned the clean, rocky slopes of Schofield Pass. "Isn't it amazing?" she said. "For all his blustering, he'd be *afraid* to come here."

Past the stream, the road down into Crystal Valley is not a road. It is a mule track carved out of a cliff, later widened to accommodate wagons. It is a narrow thirty-degree drop of jagged rocks and loose slate, and although it would be foolish to attempt in a street vehicle, it is not particularly difficult for a Jeep; in a Jeep, with care, the ride is perhaps no more dangerous than a roller coaster in an amusement park—the thrill, the danger, is mostly in the eye.

At the top of this spectacular drop, as I shifted into low gear and nosed the Jeep over the last foot of level ground, at that point of disbelief when the roller coaster first plunges into the abyss, my mother whooped. I glanced at her and caught her grinning wildly, one hand on the dash, the other balancing her flowers above her lap. Toni snickered. I pumped the brake. The Jeep bounced, shot forward, bounced. I concentrated on the rocks just past the hood, inching the Jeep down the narrow track, fifty feet, a hundred feet. My mother shifted in her seat and squinted, and then, just as I brought us to a rocking halt to check our speed, Toni tapped me on the shoulder and pointed past my chin. "What's that?" my mother said.

There, not fifty yards ahead, a chunk of cliff on the high side had collapsed and tumbled onto the road, partly blocking our way. Terrific. Why now? I thought. A month ago when I came through here, on my way to Aspen to interview a chef, the road was clear. I started forward, then stopped again, wondering if I should back out while I had a chance. Toni hopped out and trotted down the road. She stood in front of the slide for a moment, then waved us forward. When we arrived, I cut the engine and joined her to survey the damage.

"It's not too bad," Toni said. She moved a rock. "Someone's been through it already."

The slide was recent: the hole gouged into the cliff looked fresh. But Toni was right: There were shallow depressions in the loose shale—tire tracks—and most of the larger rocks appeared to have been moved against the embankment. The slide was no more than ten feet across, sloped at an angle from the cliff wall; I was sure we would make it, but for those ten feet the Jeep would be tilted precariously to the right, up on two wheels, as it were, with my mother on the down side.

I walked back to the Jeep and told my mother to climb out the driver's side. She didn't move. She wouldn't even look at me. She sat there as if frozen to the seat, fiercely gripping her flowers.

"That's ridiculous," she said. "If you're going through, I'm going through with you."

"Mother," I had to put this carefully. "Nothing's going to happen, but if it does, you'll be in the worst place . . . if it rolls."

"Oh *nuts!*" she said. "It's a piece of cake."

She's arguing, I thought. My mother never argues.

"All right," I said, "there's something else—the less weight on that side, the better." I knew this was bad before it slipped past my tongue. I tried to fix it. "Like a sailboat heeled over in a storm," I added. "All hands starboard to port!"

"Too heavy?" she said. Her goggles went up with her eyebrows. "Is that what you're saying, I *weigh* too much?"

Was she losing her mind? Was this, I wondered, the first great step into senility? Why did I have the sudden and unpleasant feeling that I was about to play the role of my father, albeit a diminished and not very convincing R. Harold Wells?

"Fine," she said. "Toni and I will lean off the port side, right behind you."

Toni came to the rescue. "Ma," she said, "four-wheelers have a code when traveling in the mountains. When there's a hazard, everyone walks except the driver."

My mother looked at her. I had never heard of this "code," and I doubted Toni had either, but my mother seemed to be turning this in her head, examining this law of the wilderness and how it applied to her, wild thing that she had become. Finally, she relented. She sighed and undid her seat belt and climbed across to the driver's side, then down. She and Toni walked to a point a few yards beyond the slide. I drove, slowly coaxing the badly tilted Jeep across, half sitting on the doorless door frame, certain that I could jump if it rolled. It didn't, of course, and a moment later we were grinding toward the bottom of the canyon and into the thick forest at the rim of Crystal Valley.

Crystal Valley is the perfect Rocky Mountain snapshot. It is a lush bowl of broad meadows flanked by steep mountains, a place of vivid green, dark to light, spruce to aspen to tall summer grass. To descend into Crystal Valley from the rocky tundra of Schofield is to experience relief, both mental and physical. Coming down lifts the spirits.

But my mother seemed to be experiencing these highs and lows in reverse. When she arrived at the airport yesterday, and until we reached Emerald Lake, her mood was polite but dull, timid. For that matter, as long as I can remember she has been that way—quiet, passive, calmly cheerful, and never argumentative, sometimes afraid and occasionally bored. And then—her strange behavior, her wild "high" at Emerald Lake and Schofield Pass. But as we crawled down from the pass, after the weird episode of having to argue her from the Jeep, I noticed that she had grown quiet again. At first I thought she was angry with me for not allowing her the thrill of two-wheeling on the edge of the cliff. But when we reached the forest, descending perhaps a thousand feet, I realized that she had somehow transformed herself into my mother again, clutching the seat with a rigid hand, staring white-faced at the road, and cordially ignoring the scenery. The more we dropped, the more she seemed to shrink, until, past old Deadhorse Mill, as we arrived at the general store in the town of Marble, she had once again assumed the passive roll of Mrs. R. Harold Wells.

I parked in front of the store. My mother carefully placed her flowers on the seat and followed Toni inside. I wanted to say something to her before she left, but I didn't know what. I even thought about returning to Crested Butte via Schofield instead of the easy way around, just to lift her mood, but I couldn't picture us grinding up that broken road, not after the trouble we'd had coming down. Toni returned, and a minute later my mother shuffled out of the store with a plastic glass of water and a straw bag over her arm. She smiled weakly and showed me the contents of the bag. "Tourist stuff," she said. Inside was a hand-carved block of wood vaguely resembling an elk, a paperweight made of polished marble from the quarry nearby, six or seven postcards. The water was for the flowers.

We turned left on Highway 133 at the north end of Crystal Valley, then climbed the paved road toward the summit of McClure Pass. Over McClure, we skirted a reservoir and turned left on a graded track that led eventually to Kebler Road and back to Crested Butte. My mother sat quietly holding her flowers, blinking behind her goggles, nodding and smiling as Toni pointed out mountains and streams and interesting landmarks. I was grateful for this. Toni was entertaining her at a time when I couldn't, partly because I didn't know these landmarks, and partly because I was, I think, still amazed and worried by her behavior in the high country. "Ma," this and "Ma" that, Toni went on, all the way home, showing we flatlanders, my mother and me, what we were missing.

Back at the house my mother padded upstairs for a bath and a nap. We had reached the edge of town at dusk, and now, close to nine o'clock, Toni and I were searching the cabinets for something to cook, or hopefully not to cook, for dinner. I was certain my mother would not appear for this meal: When we arrived and I parked in the driveway, she was stiff with fatigue, so tired she wobbled to the door, and I thought for a minute I would have to carry her into the house. She made it though, balancing her flowers in one hand and lugging her straw bag with the other, determined, it seemed, not to be a burden to us.

Toni found a package of macaroni. She riffled the refrigerator for salad things, shaking her head and telling me I'd never make it in the restaurant business. She frowned at a frozen steak and put it back, jiggled the stuck door on the breadbox and came up with a bottle of red wine, the same brand we had carried with us to Emerald Lake. "Ma's favorite," she said, searching her coat pocket for the corkscrew.

Just then, my mother appeared on the stairs. Her hair was wet, slicked back, and she wore an old coarse-knit sweater of mine, a dark green turtleneck five sizes too big—that and a pair of my jeans, the legs rolled up in thick, wide cuffs at her ankles. She looked like a tree in a pot, preened and watered. She walked into the kitchen humming, carrying her glass of wildflowers.

"I couldn't sleep," she said. Toni offered wine. My mother refused. She put the flowers on the counter and gently fluffed them with both hands. "They're wilting," she said, and then to Toni, "Do you have wax paper?"

Toni found the wax paper while I brought the iron and a pair of scissors from the utility room. My mother began, carefully trimming the stems, cutting small rectangles of paper, testing the iron with her finger. My ex-wife did this— her prom corsage, samples from our wedding, sad remnants of her sister's funeral: they were all in the huge Bible she otherwise never opened. But I had never known my mother to press flowers, not that I could remember. How did she plan to transport them to Philadelphia?

"Mind if I take your dictionary home?" my mother said. She grinned over her shoulder, a wry, wrinkled smile. "Your father will think I'm crazy, bringing these all the way from Colorado." She turned back to the counter. "But he'll like these flowers, old frustrated gardener that he is."

This was true. I once caught my father in the garden behind their house, on his knees plucking weeds, fussing in the dirt below my mother's tomato plants. He told me he had lost a golf ball.

I went for the dictionary. When I returned, Toni had moved next to my mother at the counter. They were chatting and smiling, their hands mingling and busy with Alpine forget-me-nots. I wasn't sure what came over me at that moment. Maybe it was the soft light cast by the Tiffany-style lamp above the old wooden table, the warm glow filling that slightly sagging, somewhat crooked eighty-year-old kitchen of mine. As a child, I once thought of myself as an oddly shaped segment of a difficult puzzle my parents were assembling—no matter how they turned me, I didn't fit. Over the years, though, as my edges softened, I found a place for myself. And there were moments, timeless but fleeting instants, when I saw the puzzle complete, each piece perfectly wedded to the next. I saw this now, through the doorway to the kitchen: the light, the warm pastels of that friendly room, Toni and my mother rubbing shoulders with my past and future. I wanted to hug them. I wanted to tell them what I knew would never come with words. Instead, I put the dictionary on the counter and quietly walked out of the house.

I drove to the Grubstake, a restaurant on the main street. It was Saturday night, it was crowded, but I had no trouble talking a waitress into three dinners to go. I found an empty corner and ordered a beer. The place was packed with the usual late crowd, mostly locals, a few tourists. Tomorrow, I thought, I'd bring Toni and my mother here for lunch, maybe walk around town. Monday morning, my mother would fly back to Philadelphia—I had invited her for a week, but no, she said, their house would be a mess if she stayed away that long. I caught myself smiling in my beer, playing back the scene at Emerald Lake, my mother whooping on the road down from Schofield—oh how I'd like to see my father's face!, I thought. If only he could watch this movie in my head! My mother wouldn't tell him, I knew that. She'd develop the film in her camera, show him the postcards and the flowers and the silly carved elk, tell him how "nice" Colorado was. And she'd present these souvenirs with a dry Bombay martini and a neatly folded copy of the *Wall Street Journal*, before dinner, in the den, with a discreet kiss. I wondered if she'd mention Toni, or the restaurant, or my battered Jeep and cockeyed house. And when she handed him the wildflowers, would he see the moments she had so carefully saved there?

Where Fathers Go

One summer when I was a small boy my father packed the trunk of our car and drove my mother and me to the Jersey shore. He rented a house near a town called Ship Bottom—so named, my mother was quick to explain, because a ship had run aground there and capsized in the surf. The house, a fat, tent-like structure with a steep roof, sat on the dunes above the beach. I thought this house was alive. I thought it was alive because it had a face: two round windows on the second floor, a stubby door between that led to a fire escape, and below, all across the front, a screened porch that grinned at the sea. It was the only house in view on that long stretch of white beach, and fortunately for my easily embarrassed mother, nowhere in sight was there a ship's bottom.

Every morning my father would tug me into the surf. There I would cling fiercely to his arm, my short body so powerless, so mysteriously weightless in the crashing foam. "Jump," he'd say, and I'd jump when I could. And then he'd laugh and point at the next wave and tell me to be ready, but I never was. So he'd fling me to his shoulders and stomp through the breakers snorting and ho-ho-ing like a giant, while I, giddy with laughter and shivering in the breeze, would urge him on: deeper and deeper we'd go. Once, I told him I had to go back to the house. He put me down. "Do it here, Jarrold," he said. "Everyone pees in the ocean. Even fish."

At noon, my mother would arrive and sit on a blanket beneath the largest umbrella I had ever seen, one that my father had twisted into the sand midway between the dunes and the sea. She would bring sandwiches, and when we finished eating, she'd rub oil on my shoulders and sit me in the shadow of the umbrella where I'd fall asleep.

It was after one such nap that I awoke and saw, to my amazement, a huge gray balloon above the shoreline, floating silently by, followed by another in the distance. I had acquired by then, thanks to my father, a wonderful theory to explain my new environment—what the ocean was and how the beach had become a beach—which I had related to my mother the night before. But the great balloons, big as buildings, like dark clouds on their way to a summer storm, were beyond this newly found understanding. My father called them blimps. He said blimps were flying whales—if the sea had whales, why couldn't the sky?

My mother closed her book and sighed. "Harry . . . . " she said. "He thinks sand is seagull poop and the ocean is God's bathtub." She turned to me. "They're dirigibles, Jarrold dear. They're looking for Nazi submarines."

The year was 1944.

One day, while my mother was shopping and my father had gone for a swim, a lady with fluffy blonde hair, wearing a light blue dress and carrying her shoes, walked up to me on the blanket. She pointed at my father and asked if he was my father, and when I nodded, she said "Oh." And then, before she left, she shook my hand and said her name was Millie; she said she lived in the first house behind the dunes on the next road. I told my father about her when he returned. I said she was the prettiest lady I had ever seen. I said she had big bazooms too—what he called them—and said she lived in the first house on the next road. My father thanked me. He said he'd check on it.

Earlier that year my father had been away for a long time. Until finally, just before my birthday in May, he came back to our big, ivy-covered house in Philadelphia. There were happy times when he returned, but it wasn't the same, at least not between him and my mother: My father brooded a lot, especially at night, and I could feel the tension hovering like smoke in the huge rooms of that dark house. It was my Aunt Margaret who had talked them into this vacation at the shore. "You have so little time together," she told my mother one day. "Get out of the city and make the best of it."

I had no idea what Aunt Margaret meant by that statement, but this had to be the best, I thought, this beach, this house with the smiling face. Although I wondered if my father felt the same. He had grown quieter with each day, and had started going out for walks at night, and sometimes in the morning. And then one afternoon I saw Millie again. My father told me he had found a large bed of shells that had washed up on shore, and right after lunch we set out on our expedition, my father with a pillow case and I with a carefully folded paper sack. I was excited. I particularly liked whelks, the spiral shells you could hear the ocean in; I hoped I would find one that wasn't broken. But before we had gone a hundred yards, Millie came loping off the dunes in her bathing suit.

"Look at her bazooms," I said to my father, but he hushed me. And then he did a strange thing: He held her arms and kissed her cheek and asked her what she was doing there, as if he knew her. She smiled at me. I didn't smile back. I put the paper sack on the sand and sat on it, somehow knowing I would never fill it.

A week later, Aunt Margaret and Uncle Bill came down from Philadelphia. Like my father, Uncle Bill had been away, but for so long that I hardly remembered him. He hobbled into the house on crutches and one leg, and I thought he had somehow hidden the bottom half of his other leg. My mother blinked and held her handkerchief to her mouth. My father hugged him for a long time. And when I asked Uncle Bill what he had done with his foot, he told me he had lost it in the war. I asked if he had searched real hard for it, and he said he had. I asked what war was, but he didn't answer.

That night my father stayed home. By then I knew where he went on his walks, and I think my mother did too because she sighed a lot and had stopped coming to the beach in the afternoons. Early one morning, from my bedroom window, I watched him head over the dunes toward Millie's house, and it was then that I decided I didn't like Millie. But this night, with Aunt Margaret and Uncle Bill there, I knew he wouldn't leave. And there was another reason: Something had upset my mother, something so important that she had hurried from the living room to hide her face. I found her in the kitchen, clutching an envelope, sobbing on Aunt Margaret's shoulder. This was a terrible moment. My father and Uncle Bill had retired to the darkness of the porch, and I had no idea what to do or where to go. The blackout bulb in the kitchen—another curious aspect of this "war"—cast an eerie glow on the pine-paneled walls, across the big wooden table with its flaps like wings, over the wobbly wicker chairs that made me sit lower at the table than if I were standing. This was such a friendly kitchen before, such a cheery place to gather, but now it seemed small and hostile—I was certain the knots on the walls were staring at me. I tugged at my mother's dress. I pulled her hand and made her look at me. I asked her what war was, but she wouldn't answer.

The next morning my father left with Uncle Bill and Aunt Margaret in their car. My father had the envelope in his shirt pocket. Before he left, Mother told me that Aunt Margaret had brought the mail from Philadelphia, that the envelope contained papers ordering Father to Europe to fight the Nazis. I asked where Europe was, and why, if he wanted to fight the Nazis, he didn't look for them where the blimps did, just past the waves in front of the house. She tried to smile, but there were tears in her eyes. And then, after Aunt Margaret had helped Uncle Bill into the car, my father picked me up and touched his fist to my chin and told me what he always told me when he tucked me in at night: "Close your eyes so your dreams don't fly out." I shut them hard as he walked out the door, but not to keep my dreams in, not then. I stood there for a long time, fingers in my ears, pinching my eyes so tight I could hear the wind in my head. And when I opened them he was gone, and I saw my mother sitting on the couch holding her face. I walked outside and sat on a dune.

Mother and I stayed in that house at the shore for the last week of our vacation. She took me in the ocean twice, and one afternoon when it rained we went to a movie, but mostly we took long walks on the beach. In the house, Mother read a lot and I thought a lot, especially about the Nazis. I pictured them as monsters who came from a sea called Europe and who swam up and down other people's coasts chewing on legs and looking in windows. I couldn't imagine why anyone would fight them, least of all my father. And so, on the last day before we left for Philadelphia, while my mother was napping, I packed a sandwich and set out over the dunes for Millie's. When I arrived, I knocked on the screen door, but no one answered. I went in and walked through the house. I had hoped to find my father there because Millie's had to be better than Europe, but he wasn't around. I decided to leave, and as I turned in the hall at the rear of the house, I saw a crib in the bedroom. There were baby toys on the floor, a stack of diapers on a table, tiny pink clothes on the big double bed. And on the night stand next to the bed there was a framed photograph of a man in a uniform, with one of those funny pointed hats on his head, with ribbons and medals hanging from the pocket of his jacket. Millie walked in then with her baby, and stood next to me. I asked her who the man was, and she told me he was her husband. I asked where he was, and she said he had gone to the war. I asked her what war was, and she put her baby in the crib and said, "War is where fathers go and never return."

I ran. I ran to the beach and across the dunes and all the way back to our house. I ran to my mother and woke her up. I tried to tell her that I knew what war was, but the words kept bursting in my throat.

So I Told Him

Whatever happened to crazy Stewie?" he said. "You know, Stewie, that clunky kid with glasses as thick as headlights, made his eyes look like fried eggs. The kid who laughed like a bird, tee hee, when nothing was funny, and if you told him that, he'd say *nothing* was the funniest thing he ever heard, tee hee. Remember the night he wandered into the foothills in a blizzard, and half the cops in town searched for his body the next day? And then he wandered back out with frozen fingers and icicles hanging from his nose, and nobody could pull his boots off. Said he saw Janis Joplin up on Lookout Mountain, tee hee. Yeah, Stewie, that was his name. What happened to him anyway?"

So I told him. I said Stewie melted for three days next to the stove in my kitchen, and on the fourth day he disappeared again, somewhere between the 7-Eleven and Trail Ridge Restaurant. Everyone thought he had returned to the wilderness to find Janis Joplin, but there were no footprints in the waist- deep snow on the edge of town, and no one wanted to search for Stewie again anyway, so I waited with a tub of hot water, ready to thaw him out when he stumbled in. I waited a week. Poor Stewie, I thought, stiff as a frozen fish, out there on the side of a mountain until June. And then a friend called from Tucson and told me Stewie's picture was in the newspaper there. "Tourist Leads Police To Marijuana-Eating Alligator," the article said. "Five Arrested." Stewie, my friend explained, had been dancing on the sidewalk, chanting to "Mayor Bubbah" or whoever his guru was, when a police cruiser happened by. The cop stopped, but before he could determine the nature of Stewie's flapping, a crazed woman ran out of a house nearby, pulling her hair and shouting "pig," screaming that if the cop wanted to bust someone, why didn't he bust her and leave the poor kid on the sidewalk alone. The cop chased her into the house where he found her boyfriend in the bathroom, one hand holding a sack of pot, the other halfway down the throat of a five-foot alligator in the bathtub. By the time the narcs showed up, three fugitives and a shoebox full of LSD had been flushed from the closets. Stewie was a hero and didn't know why. My friend drove him to the bus station, bought him a ticket to San Francisco.

"Funny," Luger said, "how you run into people you haven't seen for years." To this I nodded, thinking it "funny" also that this middle-aged duo, two of my old high school buddies from a younger and less complicated Denver neighborhood, had stumbled into this dark bar on Broadway that I rarely frequented. I had first seen them at the window, hands like horse blinders on their faces, peering into the smoky gloom at the cheap furniture and dirty walls, their ski sweaters rudely bright in the afternoon sun. I knew who they were, even with their double chins and shiny heads. But I didn't think they'd come in here, not this place. And then the door banged open, blown in by Bill Luger's thunderous voice, and I found myself hunched over the bar, half hoping they wouldn't recognize me, half knowing they would.

"Dwight?" Luger said. "My God it *is* you! Dwight, what're you doing here? Hey, Bradley, it's Dwight Bolles!"

Bradley Jacobson. The last time I saw him he was primping a woolly bush of bright red hair in the boys' room at school. Now his hairline had receded to the back of his neck, but he still had the curls above his ears, as red as his flushed cheeks. He looked like a circus clown in street clothes, standing behind Bill Luger as he always had. "Dwight Bolles," he said reverently, whistling through dental work I didn't remember. "Well, I'll be damned."

Luger pumped my hand. "Hell, Dwight," he boomed, "good to see you again." Back in the seventies, Luger was the hottest fullback in the city league. He was also the loudest guy in the quietest neighborhood in Denver. His voice hadn't changed, but his figure had: with the extra weight, he seemed to have grown shorter, denser, like putty settled to the floor. "What've you been doing with yourself?"

Not much, I said, and Luger studied my three-day growth. And then he did something that used to drive me nuts, me and everyone else he did it to—he stared at my forehead, grinning, as if he had spied an interesting speck of dirt there, a tea leaf of my thoughts that he and no one else could read.

Finally, Luger bought me a beer and told me he and Bradley had been shopping the neighborhood, buying new equipment, preparing for their fabulous ski weekend in Vail. Bradley Jacobson interrupted by moving between us at the bar. Bradley seemed compelled not to be left out, even more compelled to tell me about his job, as if that explained his existence, glancing frequently at my ratty jacket and scuffed sneakers, obviously hoping I wouldn't admit I was an eccentric millionaire. Strange, when we parted years ago, they had both voted me "most likely to make a fortune." And I had, in a sense, although not the way they had expected—nor could they know I had nothing to show for it, not a lot of sobriety, for one thing, and certainly not happiness. But there seemed no reason to tell them. "Yep," Bradley said, "I'm a sales rep, into women's underwear, ha ha. You think that's bad, Bill here's the doughnut czar."

"Hell yeah, Dwight, district manager of Wigwam Bakeries," Luger said, and I pictured him waddling into that glass building with the great doughnut on top, squinting at the foreheads of his pimpled employees. "But hey, Dwight, you remember Pamela, the blonde waitress at the White Spot? She's the wife now."

Oh yeah, I said, how could I forget. But the blurred image below the blonde wig in my mind was not one but many faces, some with dark eyes and tight lips, one with a permanent frown. Got any kids? I asked, knowing the answer.

"Sure," Luger said, "got five between us. Brad here and Evelyn have three girls, and me and the wife got two boys." He punched my arm. "Well hey, Dwight, you'll have to come out sometime," and with this, he fished a card from his wallet and gave me half-hearted directions to a cul-de-sac in a subdivision on the southeast edge of the city. I let Luger worry for a minute about whether or not I would show up, and then I tucked the card in my shirt pocket. He sat forward and cleared his throat.

"Say, Dwight," he said, and at this point he guffawed, slapping a pudgy hand on Bradley's shoulder. He laughed even louder, attracting the bartender. "Say, Dwight, whatever happened to crazy Stewie?"

So I told him. Him and Bradley Jacobson and the bartender. And then halfway through the story Luger interrupted with that bit about funny how you run into people you haven't seen in years, and the way he said it, I knew he didn't want to hear the rest. To Luger, people like Stewie *should* have disappeared, at least after providing him with a good laugh and a good measure of assurance that he, Bill Luger, basic middle-class jock, had always been and still was on the right track. But Bradley wanted to know more. "Did you hear from Stewie in Frisco?" he asked.

Oh, I heard from him, I said. He called me a few months later and asked me to help him with his plants. Even sent me a plane ticket. You see, Stewie always had a thing for plants, ever since he was a kid. He used to read to them, even dance with them if he thought they liked the music. Especially vegetables. Tomatoes were proud, he'd say, and rhubarb was paranoid. Strawberries were friendly but vain, and cucumbers were dangerous when aroused. And as for string beans, well, string beans were smarter than dogs, and there was nothing on the face of the earth as generous as a watermelon.

So when I arrived I found Stewie in a rented greenhouse in Marin County, surveying his happy jungle. He had four vans and four lovely female drivers and called his company Adopt-A-Plant. He also had a box of cash in the corner and a pile of coffee-stained checks on a table that he had forgotten to take to the bank. I began by throwing away the school notebook where he kept the "books," then changed the name to California Plant Rentals and started a campaign to place our green thumb in the best restaurants and largest banks in the Bay area. I had big ideas in my young head, fresh-out-of-school plans: I wanted to mechanize, automate, incorporate; I saw fields full of house plants, trucks with our giant green logo, franchise outlets across the nation; I saw an army of indoor ferns watered by a navy of uniformed gardeners. But it didn't work out—before I could expand the operation, Stewie sold it, claiming the plants were unhappy.

And then he disappeared again, this time, it seemed, for good. Me, I was out of a job and on a plane back to Denver.

Bradley shook his head. Luger sat there in the silence, slumped on a stool, but I knew he was gearing up for a verbal assault. "Heyyyy," he said finally, "great story, Dwight. Too bad he wouldn't listen to you. Crazy Stewie, he probably ended up on skid row. Say, why don't we get out of here and . . . ."

No, I said—now looking at Bradley who seemed eager for the final chapter, also not wanting Luger to get off that easy—no, Stewie didn't end up on skid row. I got a call a year ago. It was from a woman with a silky voice who told me it had taken her all morning to track me down, said she was Stewie's wife and Stewie had been thinking about me and if she sent someone to pick me up, would I come for a visit? So I flew to the Bahamas in Stewie's private plane, then on to Stewie's island in a helicopter with a towering beauty who sang silky ballads to the pilot and called herself Naomi, Stewie's mate. Stewie was in the pool when we arrived, tending the water lilies, looking younger and healthier and not nearly as silly as that snowy day he wandered into the hills. I stayed a week in Stewie's paradise, surrounded by exotic plants and noisy parrots, floating in a jade lagoon that Stewie had enclosed with a white picket fence sunk to the bottom of the sea to keep the sharks out. He didn't say much that week, except "tee hee," and I never asked him what he did to afford the lifestyle, but I couldn't help noticing the plaques and framed certificates in the study complimenting his efforts to world conservation, one a letter from the president of Costa Rica, thanking him for saving the rain forest. Just before I left, after escorting me across his island to the helicopter, Stewie bowed and kissed my hand, then told me he remembered our days in San Francisco, nearly a decade ago.

He said he sold out because of me, because I pushed when I should have flowed, because I wanted to force straight lines on a world made of circles. He said I'd die soon if I didn't stop being who I'm not, if I didn't quit doing what I couldn't. And when the helicopter took off, climbing in a long arc above the reef, I saw then what I hadn't seen when we arrived—there were no straight lines on Stewie's island. The house and pool were circular, placed neatly in the center of an ever-expanding ripple of lush gardens and manicured orchards, all of it kissing the lagoon, it too a circle where the white picket fence joined together the long bend of the shoreline. Even the heliport was part of the design, a white pad on a narrow peninsula at the far side of the lagoon, a pearl moon to a much larger circle, the island itself. So I came back to Denver, arriving at the onset of one of those gigantic summer storms that flex and rumble high above the foothills. Stewie's pilot gave me cab fare, but I decided to walk. And during that walk, with the cool, hissing rain in my face, I found myself laughing, saying tee hee, over and over until I knew what it meant. Been walking around Denver ever since, mostly in circles.

Luger had stopped listening somewhere in the middle of my description of the island. He had moved away and leaned on the bar, feigning interest, and now he was turning his beer glass in a small puddle, drawing circles only I could see. But Bradley Jacobson was staring at me, and I thought I saw him shiver, an almost imperceptible movement in his eyes, as if he had totaled every moment of the last ten years in that fraction of a second and had come up with nothing.

Luger turned and patted me on the knee. "Well, Dwight," he said, "it was good to see you again. Don't mean to be rude, but we've got some stops to make before the stores close. How 'bout it, Brad, you all set?"

"Not really," Bradley said, still looking at me. "There's plenty of time for another beer."

Luger glared at Bradley like a father about to chastise his son, and I had to admit, years ago in school, Bradley never would have said that. Rarely did anyone disagree with Bill Luger, least of all his carrot-colored shadow Bradley Jacobson.

"Whatever happened to Toni?" Bradley asked, and I heard Luger groan, a windy protest from his gut. "Last I heard, she was into mountain climbing and hang gliding and had moved to a ski town on the western slope. Whatever happened to her anyway?"

So I told him.

How You Lose

No one here knows how old this prison is. Or maybe because they work here or are confined here they do not care. The original cellhouses are gone, gone to fire, gone to attrition, gone because the Feds sued and finally closed them down. What remains is a collection of tired replacements, buildings renovated but never improved, buildings overcrowded and obsolete in a year. It is the wall that carries the oldest date—1875—stamped into the archway above the rear sally port. But even this seems vague to Alex on a good day and fraudulent on most—it was the convicts who built this wall, who cut the stone, block by block, from the quarry behind the prison. And it is their record, the countless scars of pick and hammer, that is the message, the true age of this place.

To Alex it is Old Max. Officially, it is Territorial because it was here before the state became a state, but because they no longer can tell the truth, they have changed the name from Penitentiary to Correctional Facility. And so it is Territorial

Correctional Facility. Old Max to the few who have been around long enough, when it was the only high-security prison in the state. But today there are new facilities out on the plains, two- and three-story prefabs wrapped in chain-link fences and resembling on their grassless plots misplaced schools or government warehouses. Parking garages.

Alex digs ditches. He hauls pipe and waxes floors. He and Big Stansky and Oscar Lincoln are all that is left of the old-timers—they are kept here as the labor crew, the one job that has not changed. Recently the state built a clinic up front, a hospital, and what with the other facilities opening up, they emptied Old Max of the lifers and brought in the disabled: cripples and spastics, guys with cancer and heart disease, guys with AIDS, nut cases the state mental hospital refused because they said they were crazy but not crazy enough, half of them tranquilized and barely upright. So now there is a new breed at Old Max, prisoners but hardly convicts—no loyalty, no one defending their rights, no one together. Oscar Lincoln up on a ladder shakes his head as he watches them hobble by. Stansky says they are pathetic, and even though Alex feels sorry for them he has to agree—the old days are gone.

Everywhere under the prison there are tunnels. The story goes that they were once part of a coal mine, a vast under-ground system that was here before the prison. In any case, there are tunnels, and in the winter when it snows or when the ground is frozen, where it melts you can see the outline of their route below the surface. There is the old gun tunnel, a narrow runway from the control center to the chowhall and Cellhouse One, once an approach or escape route for the guards in an emergency. There is a tunnel to Cellhouse Three, caved in now. There are steam tunnels, access to water and sewage pipes, heating ducts and electrical conduits from cellhouse to cellhouse, but now with the new wiring and plumbing, most of these are closed; of those remaining open, about the only people who go down there are junior dayshift guards whose job it is to check for cats—the prison is overrun with feral cats; in the winter months they hide from the cold in the dripping tunnels.

Alex and Stansky and Lincoln have been in the tunnels, Lincoln more than the others because he is a master plumber. But that too was years ago before they built new cellhouses at Old Max. Except they did not build new cellhouses, or they did but they built them inside the old, so that the exterior wall of the former structure is still intact, while inside, four stories high, is a new and separate building, like a box inside a box, the narrow area between the two now used as a guards' run and plumbing trap.

Which is where Stansky saw the cat. Padding along on the ground floor, not lost and not particularly curious or afraid, with no way in or out except through a locked metal door at the end of the trap. The cells open to the tiers inside, and at the rear of each cell is a thick plastic window with a view of the trap, the pipes and walkway, and depending on what cell and whether it is near one of the tall, barred windows of the old shell, a view also of the yard outside and part of the sky. And so there is light in the trap, and there was this cat, filthy white, thin and wormy, and just padding along— and according to Stansky it was not an hour before he and Lincoln began digging at the window casing in Lincoln's cell.

"Alex, you been here too long," was the first thing Stansky said when they met in the yard yesterday. Stansky is shorter than Alex but heavier, older by a decade at forty-one. Of the three, Lincoln is the youngest and the smoothest, black on black and handsome as a movie star, while Stansky is rough and loud and short-tempered, bald except for a ring of wheat-colored hair raked back and tied at the rear of his head. Stansky's nose is flat and his teeth are broken, but the most noticeable feature of his craggy face is his eyepatch—black, and slung above his ruddy cheek like a pirate's. "Alex buddy," he said, "you remember the old gun tunnel under One?"

Alex remembered. They had sealed it off down at the control center when they renovated the prison. And with it they had sealed off access to a section of ancient steam tunnels between Cellhouse One and the diagnostic unit, all along the west wall.

And then Stansky told him about the cat.

"That cat had to have come up out of the old gun tunnel. There's no other way. So I knew there was a hatch in the trap behind the cells, and some dumb cop must have left it open."

Years ago Alex and Stansky and Lincoln went out the sluice

gate—took all summer to saw the underwater bars with a rusty hacksaw, nine of them altogether, slipping one at a time into the icy water of the irrigation ditch that to this day runs through the prison. Except now there is a fence around the exit through the east wall, and the sluice itself is triple-barred. Nine of them under the wall, but Alex didn't get a city block before he was captured, soaking wet and crawling through a neighborhood yard.

And oh how you lose. It was not the freedom, so much; it was the dream. All that work, all that careful, nervous work, and then the precious moment of release, underwater, floating on his back through the pipe beneath the street outside, down the neighborhood, and up for air under a free-world sky, wanting to scream and cry and hug the first person he saw.

Even though he had nowhere to go. Alex, half his life in institutions, state-raised, his mother deserting them and his father a railroad man when away and a drunk when not. No brothers or sisters, and Alex learned to steal; learned about heroin also, got hooked when still a kid and left home, no longer took the beatings from his father. Killed a man on his eighteenth birthday, on escape from the reformatory. A house near the country club—Alex on a tip, big-time crime boss with a safe full of cash—but it was the wrong house, the wrong block, and Alex lost his head. Shot the man and his daughter because he was crazy with fear, desperate for money and the relief it would buy.

"We need you, Alex. We got to dig fast, and we need your arms." Stansky in the yard yesterday, grinning and squinting, he and Lincoln and Alex on the bleachers by the weight pile where Alex works out. "The old tunnel against the west wall, near Tower Eleven. Me and Oscar got six blocks out, three more tomorrow night and we're under the lawn outside. When we go, we got to go fast, one diggin' and two pullin' the dirt back into the tunnel. No tellin' how long before they find the hatch open."

And you lose in the punishment. When they lock you down—no privileges, no exercise, no daylight—you lose a piece of yourself, sometimes to grief but mostly to anger. After the sluice break Alex spent a year in the hole. The surly guards, the lousy food, the noise—all he wanted was the needle again, a chance to give himself away.

And Stansky had said, "Meet us here tomorrow night, after chow."

Chow is at six P.M. Count is at ten. Three, four hours to dig free. Enough, Alex figures, if all goes well.

But little time to get away. When the count comes up short there will be a search; there will be dogs, roadblocks, a hundred armed men; the steam whistle will blow and half the town will join the hunt. It will be night, and cold. There will be no food, probably for days. Alone, Alex will have his demons, but traveling with Stansky could be worse—Stansky is capable of anything, and would not care how he won his freedom.

And Stansky had said, he and Lincoln rapping Alex on the arm as they stood to leave, "Alex, old buddy, you been down too long. The river or the mountains—take your pick."

The river or the mountains. There is a highway through town, the railroad line also, but they will be watched. So it is the river heading east or the mountains to the west.

Alex climbs on the bleachers and sits. The weather is unusually mild, for winter. The evening sky is fat with clouds, and the air is heavy, muggy. Alex likes this corner of the exercise yard. Across the expanse of the ballfield and over the wall he can see the naked tops of trees, cottonwood and sycamore—there are quiet streets out there, houses where people live. To the south, beyond death row and Cellhouse Three, are more trees, in the park and along the river. And in the summer on Sundays there are families in the park, children playing, sometimes rock-and-roll or country-western bands, the scent of cook fires and barbecue in the breeze. Alex could run there, he and Stansky and Lincoln to the park, empty and dark this time of year, over the railroad tracks and to the river—and if they could stand the freezing water long enough, they could make it out of town.

For Alex, this month will be ten years. And still there are moments when it all seems unreal, in that time just before sunrise, between freeworld dreams and the reality of his cell— as if he were waking to a nightmare, day after day disbelieving his eyes, wishing he were someone else. And there are times at night when he closes his eyes and is frightened by what he sees—teeth, gleaming white fangs, the jaws of hideous monsters—when he wonders if he is losing his mind, if he is doomed and these are visions of what awaits him. And he sees the man on the floor, his skull shattered by the bullet, the girl sprawled next to him, her mouth open and eyes locked in a lifeless stare. And Alex thinks . . . more time, more years—another lifetime, perhaps they will forgive him.

It is a few minutes past six o'clock. Stansky and Lincoln are late, but now Alex sees them rounding the building. Alex knows what Stansky will say: "Alex, you been down too long. All we got to do is dig, brother. Five, six feet, we're home."

But for Alex there is no home. There is no one and nowhere. And the thought jars him, as though he had realized it for the first time. Watching Stansky and Lincoln approach, he is aware of a pressure in his chest; already he is submerged in the fast-moving river, disoriented and out of air. This is how you lose, he thinks, this is the final loss: Trapped, humiliated for years, you carry it with you—the guilt, the anger, your life twisted tight around your neck—out of prison and you carry it like a disease. And there is no one.

Lincoln may make it. Stansky will rob the first bank he sees, Alex knows this, but Oscar Lincoln has people in L.A. Lincoln, shaved head, tall and gangly and who with his feathery voice and blazing smile is fond of saying to Alex, "You all right, for white folk," has offered more than once to help Alex with a place to stay if they ever get out, but Alex has not much considered this. No, he would probably go it alone, down the river and then across the plains to a nearby city, steal a car. Steal clothes, a car, move from city to city, back on the edge of things. Even Lincoln who has a home cannot go there, not if he intends to remain free or alive.

Alex steps down from the bleachers. Stansky is grinning, shuffling casually across the exercise yard, while Lincoln at his side is his usual cool self, even though the hitch is missing from his stride. Alex waits, standing straight to greet them. He must decide. He is aware that he belongs here; he knows that the difference lies close to his heart and that he must not waste the days and months and years he has left, running. Or he can leave; he can dig free under the wall tonight, hit the river, and then go with Lincoln or set off on his own—certainly the prison has changed, and without Stansky and Lincoln he will be alone here, a freak among freaks. And there is this: He is afraid to leave but even more afraid to stay—he may die here; he may come to the end knowing what he has missed, or worse, knowing what awaits him—somehow he must rid himself of these visions; more than anything he must erase what he sees when he closes his eyes.

The Ride

A nyway," Dwight says, "I'm hitchhiking in this blizzard on Highway 50. I don't know where I am. I'm near Gunnison, I think, and the temperature's dropping and the wind's blowing, and just as I'm sure I'll freeze, along comes this guy in a junkyard Buick. Man, I'm so happy I cry when he stops. I mean, it must be five below and this is the first car I've seen in an hour!"

"So I'm shivering all over and yanking at the door handle and telling this guy, 'Mister, you are HEAV-EN-SENT,' when I see there's something weird about this car. Like, there's no difference between the inside and the outside. I mean, there's snow two feet deep on the front seat, and this guy looks like the Abominable One himself, wearing goggles and a ski mask, ice all over him. I can't believe it, there's no glass in this bomb, no windshield even!"

Toni opens the front door. She kicks snow off her boots and steps into the hall with a paper sack at her chest. Jarrold gets up to help, but she marches past and into the kitchen.

"Toni," Jarrold says, "you'll never guess what happened to Dwight on the way up here."

"Oh?" she says, shedding her parka and digging in the bag. She removes a six-pack of beer, cans of tuna, a loaf of bread. This is what she went out for, beer and tuna, apparently Dwight's favorite food. When Dwight showed up a half-hour ago she took his jacket and told him to sit, as though she saw him every day. Then she went to the store.

Jarrold fetches a beer for Dwight. Jarrold rarely drinks beer in the winter, but it looks good so he opens one for himself. Besides, this is a special occasion: Jarrold has heard about Dwight but hasn't met him before—Dwight was Toni's first lover, although Toni never said that exactly. But she and Dwight were a number in high school and then on and off for nearly a decade after that. Just last week she happened to mention to Jarrold that there had been only two men in her life—Dwight, and of course, Jarrold. So this is a special occasion, although Jarrold isn't sure if it is especially good or especially bad. He offers Toni a beer, but she declines. He tells her about Dwight's ride on Route 50 this morning, the blizzard that somehow missed Crested Butte, the car with no windows. "Really," she replies, deadpan.

"So where'd he drop you off?" Jarrold calls from the kitchen. He holds out Dwight's beer—he wants Dwight in the kitchen so Toni can hear the rest of this story. "You make it to Gunnison?"

Dwight gets off the couch and pulls his wool shirt out of

his jeans. He shuffles through the doorway and stands next to Toni, and Jarrold can't imagine them ever having been together—Toni is tall and lithe, with pale, lightly freckled skin, long blonde hair, and delicate blue eyes. Dwight, however, is chunky and wide. His pocked and weathered face, framed by a dark, bushy beard, seems too small for his head, and he has a tendency to hunch his shoulders and sway as he walks, like a bear.

"Yeah, we made it to Gunnison," Dwight says. "Some ride, though. Me, I'm down on the floor because the heater's on. But the radio's blasting too, country-western, and I don't know which is worse, the cold or the music. Finally we slow down, so I get up to see where we are. All this time the guy hasn't said a word, but now he wipes snow off his mask-hole and asks where I'm going. 'Crested Butte,' I tell him. 'North of here thirty miles.' I figure he's heading west on Route 50 and this is where I get off, downtown Gunnison. Which is fine with me because I got to get warm in a gas station or a store or somewhere with windows."

"But the guy keeps going. I'm about to say something, when all of a sudden he pulls to the curb and stops in front of a bank. 'I'll run you up there,' he tells me—like Crested Butte is on his way, like thirty miles in this storm is nothing. Then he reaches under his chin and pulls his ski mask off, goggles and all. It's Jack Nicholson. I can't believe it, but there he is, Jack Nicholson, wispy hair flying back from the wings of his big forehead, smiling that what-do-you-think-of-that! smile of his. He chuckles, heh heh, and drops the mask on the seat. And then, in slow motion, he makes a gun out of his hand, screws up his face in a one-eyed squint, and takes aim at the building. 'But first,' he croaks, 'I gotta go rob this bank.' "

Toni hands Dwight a plate. On it is a tuna sandwich, a small salad, some chips. Dwight takes a long pull on his beer. Jarrold is waiting for Toni's reaction, but already she is back at the counter, hands whirling in the sink as if Dwight's headline story were everyday news. Suddenly Jarrold feels foolish: This must be a joke, he thinks—the punch line is about to fall. But then he is not so sure: Toni is acting strangely, and there is nothing in Dwight's bearing to suggest he is joking. It dawns on Jarrold that Dwight is some sort of misfit—a compulsive liar maybe, a freak hallucinating on drugs—which makes him a little angry: at Dwight, at Toni, maybe at both of them. If Dwight's wacko, why didn't Toni warn him? Why didn't she interrupt, or at least pass him a clue? At the moment Jarrold sees no way out—Dwight is eyeing him, sandwich in one hand and beer in the other.

"So . . . this fellow who looked like Jack Nicholson," Jarrold says. "Did he, in fact, rob the bank?"

Dwight smiles. He puts his beer on the table and takes an enormous bite of the sandwich, at least half of one half; part of it hangs from the corner of his mouth until he stuffs it in with a dirty thumb. He chews for a minute, then makes room in his mouth to speak.

"Hard to figure. If he went in to rob it, why take the mask off, with a face everybody'd recognize?"

Jarrold has no answer for this. Dwight swallows, then reads the label on the beer can. Jarrold doesn't know what to say. Anything he does say, he realizes, will either provoke a confrontation or sound phony and condescending, so he decides to remain quiet. The silence is embarrassing. Dwight pushes chips in his mouth and crunches loudly, until finally Toni dries her hands with a dish towel and asks him if he needs another beer, which he does. She looks at Jarrold and taps her watch. "We have a restaurant to run," she says. Which—and for the rescue Jarrold silently showers her with gratitude—they do.

This restaurant is located at the ski area nearby. Crested Butte—the town itself—is little more than a one-main-street village, once a mining camp high in the Colorado Rockies. But the ski area at Mount Crested Butte is a thriving community in itself, a spreading cluster of woody condos and semiswanky shops nestled at the base of the mountain. There is the usual assortment of chalet hotels and casual restaurants, but of the latter, only one that serves live jazz in the cocktail lounge every Saturday and Sunday, the one that Toni and Jarrold opened the week before Christmas, only three months ago.

It is all new to Jarrold, this restaurant, this town, these mountains. A year ago he was still in Philadelphia, still reeling from an agonizing divorce, still vice president of Penn Chemical and barely able to drag himself to the office each day. He had been to Colorado once before on a ski vacation, liked what he saw. So he took a chance, sold what he couldn't carry, moved out here for good. It wasn't easy, changing worlds, pioneering this restaurant with his last dollar. The irony was that his wife, a fitness instructor with a new job and a new boyfriend in Florida, said she divorced him because he was too sensible, too stuffy, forever bound to his narrow, tedious routine; she claimed he'd never leave Philadelphia or his father's chemical company. He got the idea for the restaurant from a waitress at another place in town, a woman known around Crested Butte more for her abilities as a mountaineer and a skier and as the first person to hang glide off the top of Mount Crested Butte; she also happened to live in the log cabin next to the old Victorian house he had bought. Last spring Jarrold leased the property at the ski area, hired a crew to build the restaurant. Come October, Toni quit her waitress job, sold her cabin, and moved into the back room of his house; a month later, before he could hire her to run his classy new cafe with the jazzy bar, she married him.

And so Toni is new to him also. He knows little of her past and she knows little of his. But that seems part of the lifestyle here: the mountains welcome those who start anew, who leave their stale histories in the cities below. Toni grew up in Iowa with a hairdresser mother and an endless supply of substitute fathers; they moved to Denver, and all through high school what she wanted more than anything was for her mother to quit drinking, for the two of them to settle down and lead a normal life. And yet in school Toni was attracted to the likes of Dwight, the guy who would never learn the meaning of the word stability. He graduated but hit the road, and years later Toni finally quit waiting and moved up here to get away, to find a job and buy a place. And all the while, Dwight pounded the highways, occasionally sending a postcard from one or another obscure corner of the world.

It is Saturday. The restaurant will be packed tonight. As usual, Toni is ready before Jarrold is; as he steps out of the bathroom she is tying her hair in a pony tail, flipping it off the back of her sweater and checking herself in the mirror. He tells her, as he tells her every day, that she looks better than yesterday. Usually this brings a smile or a smart remark, but today she picks at a blemish on her face and curses when it bleeds. "So what is Dwight? . . . " he says, pausing to get the words right for a question he isn't sure he wants answered. But before he can continue she shrugs and says loudly, "Dwight's Dwight," then walks around him and into the bathroom.

Jarrold hears Dwight rummaging in the refrigerator downstairs. The heater kicks in, adding a hiss to the thickening silence in the bedroom. Toni walks out and stops at the vanity, makes a face at herself and looks at him via the mirror.

"I don't know what to say. You mean what does he do? I don't know what he does. Sometimes he works, sometimes he travels. . . . He hitchhikes a lot because he hates buses and doesn't have a car. It's hard to say what he is because it's not like he *is* a lawyer or *is* a mailman or *is* whatever—he isn't really anything. He's just Dwight."

Jarrold considers this, and says, "You criticizing or defending him?"

She sits on the bed. She takes a shaky breath and sighs. "You know when I saw him last? Three years ago. I'm in the hospital with appendicitis. Dwight appears in the middle of the night stinking of farm animals, tells me he rode all the way from a ranch in Wyoming—on a horse."

"Jack Nicholson in a junkyard Buick," Jarrold says.

She nods, walks to the closet, and finds her boots, then pads to the dresser for socks. There are tears in her eyes when she returns.

"Why does he upset you?"

She shakes her head and doesn't answer.

"You want him out, I'll throw him out," Jarrold says.

She blinks and wipes her cheek with a sock. Although he is glad he said it, Jarrold wonders how he would throw Dwight out of the house—Dwight must have a fifty-pound advantage, and none of it appears to be fat.

"No, it's not like that," Toni says, sitting on the bed again. "It's just that sometimes I catch myself believing his stories, or wishing they were true. Sometimes I even wonder if he's right and I'm wrong, like I've got all these sophisticated and elaborate plans for scaling the mountain, and Dwight's out there soaring in the clouds, landing on top whenever he wants. . . . Anyway, he won't be here long. He's checking on me, making sure I'm okay."

Defending him, Jarrold decides. But why? Because she misses him, or misses what she thinks he represents in her? Except Dwight's a liar, and the trouble with a liar is that he creates his own reality, and it is always better than your own. So maybe she isn't defending him. Maybe she's defending herself. Even Jarrold feels threatened—this was his big move: the mountains, the restaurant, another shot at marriage. And now Dwight arrives with his nutty fiction to show them up, as if to prove they had simply dragged along their old routines, combined them, and set them up in a new but same old place.

The doorbell rings. As Jarrold reaches the bottom of the stairs, Dwight opens the door. Hank, a friend, stands on the porch. Hank squints at Jarrold, then does a double-take at Dwight, slowly raising a hand to point at Dwight's chest. Finally, with a "Wow," he snaps his fingers.

"Dwight! *Isla Mujeres.* What was it—damn!—five years ago?" Hank pumps Dwight's hand and steps inside. "Well I'll be. . . . You still got those leaky skiffs you rented out to tourists?"

Hank, who is six-four and weighs two-sixty, has Dwight by the shoulders now. He turns to Jarrold. "This guy saved my ass in Mexico. Snuck me off the island before the cops got me, drunk and out of order I think it was." To Dwight he says, "You ever find that Spanish galleon? What about that pretty señorita? Hey, how do you know Jarrold and Toni, anyway?"

Dwight explains that Toni is an old friend, that years ago they went to school together. Hank is amazed almost to tears. Hank is a bartender at a local pub; he is here because Jarrold offered him a job at the restaurant; today Jarrold will show him the layout, and Hank will decide by Monday. Dwight visits the kitchen and returns with the last two beers. Toni comes down the stairs just as Jarrold pulls his coat on for a quick trip to the store.

A case of beer. This will be Jarrold's donation to the reunion. He and Toni must leave soon, but there is no need for Hank to see the restaurant today; tomorrow will be just as good. Driving into town, Jarrold wonders about Dwight's exploits in Mexico. What happened to his boats? The pretty señorita? What about that Spanish galleon? And Hank—who is older and half again Dwight's size and who resembles everyone's big brother—all the while at the door Hank was gushing and waving his hands and practically kowtowing as if Dwight were a dreamworld idol from the past . . . somehow this brings to mind a magazine article Jarrold once read about Jack Nicholson's house in Aspen, how Nicholson would spend much of his time there when not in Hollywood or on the road making a film. Aspen—Jarrold need not remind himself but does anyway—is not far from Crested Butte, only one mountain range away.

Back at the house Toni greets him at the door with a familiar smirk. Jarrold once had mixed feelings about this smirk, partly because he never knew what she was thinking when it appeared, and also because it created in him the immediate and quite physical desire to carry her upstairs and find out. Now, however, he knows it as one of her private and more comfortable smiles, and in this case he interprets it as an expression of something resolved, evidence that she has somehow decided, in the ten minutes that he has been gone, that she is better off as a scaler than a cloud-hopper. Probably because of Hank, the way Hank was fawning at Dwight, magnifying Dwight's lies. It also occurs to Jarrold, by the way she takes his arm as he steps into the house, that she has never smiled this way at anyone else, that this wonderful smirk is reserved for him—but now Hank is between them, grinning and yanking the case of beer from Jarrold's hands, tugging him to the living room. "Oh man," Hank says, guffawing, "you got to hear this!"

Dwight, who is on the couch, lifts his jacket from a nearby chair. Jarrold notices that he has pulled his boots on and donned his wool cap. Dwight takes a beer from Hank, tilts it to his mouth, and winks at Jarrold. Jarrold knows what the story is—Dwight didn't have to wink—but somehow this gesture clears the air and binds Jarrold to what will follow: He is eager to hear the conclusion. Toni sidles up and takes his hand.

"So he comes out of the bank," Dwight says. "He's swinging this money bag that's tied around his wrist. I think, damn, maybe he did rob it, and now we're both going to jail—except he'll get out because of who he is, and I'll rot because of who I'm not. So I'm looking around, waiting for an alarm or a siren or somebody to shoot us, when he calmly slides into the car and hands me the bag. I've got to check inside, so I do. It's stuffed with money. There must be, oh, forty, fifty grand in there, mashed in by the fistful. I say to him, 'Why rob a bank, rich guy like you?'

" 'Rob it? What made you think thaaat?' he says—you know, with the big toothy smile and that Jack Nicholson drawl—'You think I'm craaayzee?' Then he tells me he's buying a ranch near Crested Butte and the owner wants part down in cash. So he's bringing him cash.

"We drive north out of Gunnison, on our way to Crested Butte. It quits snowing and the sun comes out and I'm beginning to get used to the wind in my face. I'm even beginning to like this weird old car. I say, 'You drive a piece of junk like this in Hollywood?'

"He laughs and says no, his four-wheeler broke down coming off Monarch Pass, and some kid loaned him the clunker and the goggles. Then he tells me about his house in Aspen, how he's tired of all the rich and ridiculous there, how it must be great out here where it's quiet.

" 'So what will you do on this ranch,' I say, 'run cattle?'

" 'Yaks,' he tells me. 'You know—those hairy cows from Tibet. Thought I'd start a yak butter business. Maybe put up some yurts and have yak treks in the mountains.'

" 'Oh,' I say. And then we get to this ranch, which is beautiful, and the rancher, he's all uptight because Nicholson is late and the real estate man and the notary guy have already left and now he has to get them back out there. So Nicholson says to me, 'C'mon, I got time to run you into town.'

"So we cruise into Crested Butte. I tell Nicholson I'm here to visit a friend but don't know where she lives, so we find a bar where I can ask some questions. The waitress tries to be cool, but I know she's gaga over Nicholson—she even shoots me a look like I'm his sidekick or a stunt man or somebody important. We order a beer and Nicholson says, 'You know anything about ranching?' I say, 'I know a lot about ranching.' He thinks for a minute, and says, 'Tell you what, I'll drop you at your friend's and come back in two hours and set you up with a job that's probably better than the one you got.' I think for a minute, and tell him, 'I don't have a job'—at which he smiles and then I smile and he pays the tab and we walk out to the car. Then we find the house and he lets me off on the corner . . . . "

Dwight lifts the beer can to his mouth and guzzles, shifting his eyes from Hank to Toni. When he finishes, he grins broadly and shrugs.

" . . . and here I am."

The silence, as they say, is deafening. Hank gawks at Dwight, Toni stares at the floor, and Jarrold seems to be caught somewhere between competing realities. Then everyone moves at once—Hank grabs another beer, Toni tells Jarrold they are late for work, and Dwight checks his watch, announces that Jack will soon be by to pick him up.

Toni and Jarrold prepare to leave. Hank cannot believe they are deliberately passing up the chance to meet Jack Nicholson, restaurant or no restaurant. Toni kisses Dwight on the cheek. As she opens the door, she tells him to take care of himself, in a voice that reveals she has played this scene before, with that hollow sigh of exasperation that says it will be years before they meet again, and maybe just as well. Dwight smiles and thanks her for lunch. He shakes Jarrold's hand. "See you around," he says.

When Toni wishes to think instead of talk, she bows her head. She does not gaze at the horizon or lock herself in a room somewhere; she looks down, at the floor or at her lap. There is no one emotion associated with this: Jarrold has watched her read a book without turning a page after a good phone call from her mother, and then a day later burn a hole in the rug in a controlled fit of anger over a bounced check from an obnoxious customer. And so, in their Jeep, on the way to the ski area, Jarrold drives and Toni studies her boots. It is a five-minute ride to the restaurant, not much time, Jarrold realizes, for Toni to put her thoughts in order. What a strange person, this Dwight. How can he function with his fantasies? How, Jarrold wonders, has he avoided one or another form of institutional confinement thus far in his life?

Part way up the hill there is a bend in the road. From this high point there is a good view of the town for those who are traveling in the opposite direction, coming down from the ski area. Jarrold has a habit of checking the rearview mirror here, partly to see the traffic behind and partly for a passing glance of the toy buildings and bug cars in the white rows of their snow-covered village. The last snowfall was ten days ago, so that many of the roofs and all of the vehicles now show their original skin. Which is why he so readily notices the car in the mirror as it turns from the highway and into town—it is covered with snow, at least a foot on the rear deck, as though having recently emerged from a blizzard. Toni sits up as Jarrold pulls to the side of the road and stops. "What's wrong?" she asks, looking back to see what he sees. But the car is gone. In its place, or at least where it should be, there is a small black truck. Jarrold waits, scanning the highway and the town, but there is no sign of the snow-packed car; the street in front of their house is empty.

Toni looks at him. She smirks, and again Jarrold wonders what she is thinking. But this time there is a playful glint in her eyes, and suddenly he realizes she suspects him of highway lechery: once before, although not exactly here, he stopped and pawed her in a moment of laughter and desire. Now the smirk widens to a grin, and she throws her hands up in mock defense. When he reaches for her, she bats his arm away and pounces on him, cackling. It is hard to drive this way, but he manages to find first gear and coax the Jeep up the shoulder. Before he turns onto the highway, he checks the mirror one final time. There are no junkyard Buicks in sight.

And yet he could have sworn. . . .

The Interview

Socorro, New Mexico. We left from the airfield on the edge of town. The plane was a stubby twin, larger and more rugged looking than most, with oversize tires on a sturdy tricycle landing gear. There were trails of black oil on the engine nacelles, and on the fuselage below the cabin windows the paint was worn thin or missing altogether as if it had been sandblasted off. A T-bone, he called it, an ancient Beech, and with the cabin stripped of seats and stinking of sweat, I had the impression I was climbing into an old ranch truck, not an airplane. We took off noisily and hung a right, labored into a moonless sky above the freeway south to Truth or Consequences, and twenty minutes later, at ten thousand feet and temporarily satisfied that this junker wouldn't fall back to earth in a storm of nuts and bolts, I relaxed a little, dug out a pen, and held my notebook under the glow of the instrument panel.

"Who pays you?" I said. "The refugees?"

"No. The church does. The refugees have already paid by

the time they reach me." He leaned forward and tapped a fuel gauge that was reading empty.

"Paid who?" I said. "Mexicans?"

"Yeah. Most of the refugees are from the camps in Chiapas along the Guatemalan border. They work, save what they can, pay their last *quetzal* or *peso* to a Mexican syndicate that shuttles them north."

"What about you? How much do you make?"

He glanced at me. "Enough."

"A flat rate? By the head?"

"Five-hundred a head. Plus expenses, gas, and repairs."

Repairs . . . and I wondered how much it cost to keep this dinosaur, this pterodactyl, in the air. There were no fancy avionics on this thing either, no color radar or loran—I wasn't even sure if the navigation equipment worked because he hadn't touched the radio since we left; he seemed to be flying by sight, by the occasional ranch light below, holding the orange haze of El Paso out the left window.

"That's not exactly a bundle, is it? For risking your life?"

He sniffed. He had removed his drugstore sunglasses at the airstrip in Socorro, but I still couldn't tell the color of his eyes—blue, I guessed, although they were large and forlorn and looked gray in the dim light of the cockpit.

"Beats working," he said. "Five, six trips a month, it adds up."

"And the adventure?"

"Yeah, there's adventure, excitement, all that. But it gets old after a while. Sometimes it's like driving a bus, down and back."

I looked at his skinny arm, the hand with the long, knobby fingers spread across the thigh of his ragged jeans, knuckles and nails black with grease as though he had recently repaired an engine. Suddenly I wished I were sitting on a parachute, or had it strapped to my chest, or wherever it was the old fighter pilots used to wear them.

"Where'd you get this plane?" I said.

"Found it in Tucson. Rebuilt it and brought it home. My dad flew one of these."

"Your dad?"

"Yeah, he flew dope. Up this same corridor."

Somehow I couldn't picture him with a father. I didn't see him as an orphan, but as tall and leathery as he was I couldn't imagine him ever having been small, or ever having answered to a parent.

"Where is he now?" I said.

"He isn't. He bought it down south, crashed on takeoff. Him and another guy in a converted D-18, and somebody must have rigged the fuel line wrong from an auxiliary tank in the nose. When the gear came up it exploded . . . . "

I waited, expecting him to continue, but he lifted a flashlight from under the seat and aimed it at his watch, then looked out to his left. "Mexico," he said.

There was nothing below us, no lights, no indication of

a border. My feet were cold, and I wished I had worn heavier socks.

"So tell me, how did you lose your teeth?" I said.

He smiled, pulled his lips back over that empty space, and suddenly seemed older by a decade.

"My second flight down. I had a 182 then, a little single-engine Cessna, got caught in a crosswind on approach and stuck it in the bushes next to the strip. The Mexicans loved it. They found my teeth the next day embedded in the padding on the instrument panel. Sawed that plane in a thousand pieces and carried it off on burros."

"No police?"

"Not out there."

Out where? I wondered, imagining an army of donkeys with airplane parts strapped on their sides, descending a steep and slippery trail in a jungle fog.

"No other accidents?"

He shook his head.

"Because I hear a lot about smugglers getting killed, flying too low, running out of fuel, whatever."

"Yeah, well, when things go wrong in an airplane, they go wrong fast. You don't have a lot of time to think, so whatever you do has to be right. Especially if there isn't much air between you and the ground."

"You know of others?" I said.

"Sure. Well, like my dad. He flew with a bunch of guys they called the Clovis Air Force, from out around Clovis and Tucumcari. There were fourteen of them, and now half are gone."

"Dead?"

"Dead."

He pointed the flashlight at the compass, then at an un-lit gauge.

"Tell me more about your dad," I said.

"Like what?"

"Anything. Where he was from, how he got along."

"I didn't know him too well. Most of what I do know I learned from his friends or my mother. He was from back east originally, and I guess he was a private cop before he became a smuggler. He never married my mom, but he never messed around with other women either. He just wasn't home much because he was always on some kind of mission."

"A mission?"

"Yeah, flying pot up from Guerrero or TV sets down to Guadalajara. Stuff like that."

"Did you know this was happening? I mean, what he did for a living?"

"Well, yes and no. I was pretty young, seven or eight at the time. But I knew he was doing something illegal, or at least something I wasn't supposed to talk about with other kids. Although back then he was sort of a hero, flying grass up for the hippies. There was never any coke or heroin or any of that shit."

"And your mother went along with it?"

"Sure, she was a hippie herself, an L.A. girl, went to the love-ins, all that."

I said, "Is that how you got the name Merk?"—in San Antonio when the church group told me I'd meet their pilot, the picture that had immediately come to mind was that of a gray-haired airline captain, handsome and suave. But the pilot who showed up at my motel door in Socorro was young, late-twenties, gawky like a teenager and sporting a lopsided, toothless grin, offering his hand and calling himself Merk, M-E-R-K.

He eyed me, an expression of disgust on his face that I took as a plea to drop the subject.

"Let me guess," I said, "You're a sixties kid, a member of the 'Moon-Unit' generation, so your mother named you Mercury. Only, you changed the 'c' to a 'k' to clean it up."

"Not bad."

"And now whenever someone asks you about it, it brings back all the stupid nicknames your grade school buddies taunted you with, names you thanked God your mother didn't name you, but it hardly mattered that she didn't."

He laughed, and I caught a good profile of his face against the reflected light on the side window—the furrowed brow and long, sloping nose, the wide mouth pulled tightly into the hollow of his cheeks and maybe too easily mistaken as a friendly smile, and I wondered: How many wise-ass kids had had an eye blackened for calling him one of those other names—Jupiter or Uranus maybe, or worse, Pluto?

"Where is she now?" I asked.

He hesitated.

"Is she alive?"

"Yeah, she's alive. She doesn't live in this country, by her own choice, but she's fine. Got herself a house in Mexico, plenty of friends, all she needs."

"Why Mexico?"

He sat back, parting his legs to slide his knees under the panel. "She doesn't like it here. She figures she isn't welcome, all those years with my dad, the Man following her around, watching the house. She never really came back from that whole sixties thing. You know, when Leary said, 'Turn on; tune in; drop out,' she did. Thing is, she never dropped back in."

He checked his watch again, eased the throttles back and pushed the nose over into a gentle descent. I asked where we were headed and he said, "Tarahumara country, the Sierras west of Chihuahua." The temperature in the cabin had fallen maybe twenty degrees, and the summer windbreaker I had on wasn't doing much to keep me warm.

"So you do this for money," I said.

"That's right."

"No particular feeling for your cargo?"

He ran his hand through his spiky crew cut, ignoring the question.

"How did you get started?" I asked.

"Someone approached me. It was a good deal, so I took it."

"Why not drugs? You could make ten, twenty times what you're making now."

"Dope's out, or haven't you heard? All the good pot is grown in this country now, so what you're talking about is cocaine, and cocaine's out. Anyway, yeah, I could make twenty times the money, but I could also do twenty years in the slammer, so it's hardly worth it, is it?"

"I guess not." I said, "But what about the illegals you're bringing in, all the U.S. jobs you're giving away, the tax money we pay to take care of these people?"

He bristled. "You believe that horseshit? These folks don't take U.S. jobs, they do the jobs nobody'll take. You know something? This is the only country with cops patrolling its border, the only country I know with a 'Border Patrol.' The U.S. of A., land of the free, give me your huddled masses—with cops and fences along the border, and now they're building a wall, for Godsake, just to keep the masses from taking our jobs."

"Then what do you think is the real reason?"

"Elitism. Jingoism. Painted over with all the rhetoric about inner city social problems and economic hardships, when in fact we're misdirecting billions every day." He glanced over. "I don't know, racism maybe."

"Which means you take the position of the church, or Peace Without Borders, or whoever you work for."

"I don't work for anyone. Peace Without Borders pays the bill, that's all. And no, I don't take their position—they're pretty much convinced most of the people coming from Salvador and Guatemala are political refugees. I'm not so sure. As far as I'm concerned, they're here for the same reason I am—money. Which is a damn good reason, because money makes it work. Everyone works for money."

"So it comes down to money again."

He sighed, then hitched his mouth into an exasperated sneer. "How'd you get to me, anyway?"

"I wrote a book about the homeless," I said. "It did well, so now I'm writing one about the refugee problem."

"And?"

"And I heard about a group in Texas that was smuggling refugees. I went there and met them, said I wanted to travel with a family of illegals, enter the country with a 'coyote' and then ride with them to wherever they were going."

"So the group you met was Bernie."

"A friend of a friend," I said.

"And you spent a month in San Antonio while they checked you out. Bernie and Elisa and every last one of them living underground like spies or criminals."

"Peace Without Borders," I said.

"Right. Church people, and our own government's got half of them in jail and the other half on the run. But you know what? There's money backing that organization, serious bucks, because a lot of people support what they stand for."

"Which is how they afford someone like you? Instead of your basic border rat?"

"Hey, there's guys charge twice what I do, and put illegals through the worst kind of hell. March them out in the desert, rape the women, starve them half to death—then run off and leave them if they even hear about a cop within fifty miles. What kind of way is that to enter the promised land?"

I didn't answer, and he turned his head and gazed at me with those big liquid eyes. I wanted to ask him about his motives again, the money behind it all, but I held it.

"So you're writing a book," he said.

I nodded.

"How much you think you'll make?"

"Enough."

He smiled, and I thought: *Touché*. Although what I didn't tell him was that I had offered a percentage to Peace Without Borders, that I, or rather my publisher, had already paid a hefty chunk for the story, cash up front. Enough to pay for coyote Merk's next five or six trips, at least.

He reached to the floor next to his seat, turned a switch for an auxiliary fuel tank. When he sat up, I said, "How long have you been doing this?"

"Almost a year now."

"Would it be a stupid question if I asked if you had ever done it legally, at least on the way down, stopped to clear customs?"

"Yeah, pretty stupid."

"How about coming back, you ever been chased?"

"You mean by a Mohawk?"

"Mohawk, Blackhawk, whatever they're using."

"Not yet."

"Don't you think that's strange, with all the radar surveillance along the border, AWACS, the aerostat balloons?"

"Yeah, maybe. But they never caught my dad either. They didn't have the balloons and all the military help back then, but they had AWACs and Citations, and he had a hell of a lot more heat on him than I do. Every time he made a preflight he found the plane bugged. Got so he'd take the transponder out and put it in his car before he took-off, reinstall it when he got back." He chuckled, and tugged on his nose.

"What's so funny?"

"That he never got caught."

I waited, and said, "You want to tell me why?"

He raised his eyebrows and peered at me as if over a pair of reading glasses. "Probably the same reason I've never been chased."

"Which is?"

He laughed. "No, no way. I tell you now, you'll jump out when we land and walk back to the border. Then what would you do with all those notes you're taking, write half the story?"

We had dropped only a thousand feet from our cruising altitude when he lowered the flaps and began a wide turn to the left, his face at the side window. We circled twice that way, Merk craning his neck and mumbling to himself, until suddenly he sat up, lowered the gear, and shoved the throttles forward. A minute later he made a hard left, then another, and I saw what he had been lining up on: a few faint rings of light, six in all, two in the middle and two at each end of the strip. They were lanterns, he told me, flashlights—the beams aimed at the ground to produce the eerie, elliptical shapes, recognized from the air only by someone who knew what they were.

He brought it in as though planting it on a carrier deck, steep and nearly in a stall, and the instant we hit he cut the landing lights, rolled to a stop at the far end, and shut down the engines. One by one the lanterns disappeared, and as I unbuckled myself, someone knocked at the cabin door. I shuffled back to open it, suddenly feeling queasy and light-headed, a little airsick now that we had landed.

He was a boy, no more than fourteen, wearing a straw sombrero and a dark leather jacket, holding one of the lanterns and shining it at the steps as I lowered them. An older look-alike came out of the darkness behind him and greeted me with a cold stare, just as Merk called their names from the cockpit. The boy was Joaquin; his father was don Guillermo; they were the landing crew, part of the syndicate that transported the refugees north.

The air was cooler than in Socorro, so I assumed we were on a high mesa, and the breeze carried with it the scent of pine, spiced with wood smoke. But as much as I wondered where we were I had no desire to inspect the surrounding darkness. If I was uncomfortable in the plane, at least there I had my work to keep me tethered to reality; stepping outside into this lightless and alien night was unnerving—I kept thinking that I couldn't speak the language, that without Merk I'd never get out of here. Guillermo left, and the boy offered me a plastic jug, the contents of which reeked of something fermented—*tesquina*, Merk called it, a local maize beer—and I passed, hoping I hadn't offended anyone, but opting to quench my thirst from the canteen in the cockpit.

Guillermo brought them to the rear of the plane. There were six: three men, a woman, and a young girl, the woman with a baby strapped to her back in the folds of a *rebozo*. They were Indians, the men thin and frail-looking, the woman with tiny, hidden eyes and a wide nose. The men wore *huaraches* with automobile-tire soles, western-style shirts and pants that, although wrinkled and dirty, seemed new, not yet washed for the first time. The woman and the girl also wore *mestizo* clothes—blouses and skirts—and someone had dressed the girl in a pink store-bought sweater; she stood there trembling, staring at the plane, clutching a corner of her mother's scarf as though it were the last thread not only of her lost home but of her short life.

In the plane they curled up at the rear of the cabin, and Merk had to coax them forward, spreading a blanket for them where their combined weight was closer to center. I could smell their fear, and wondered if it was because of the plane— surely this was their first flight—or because of a future they had probably heard about but couldn't possibly imagine.

Merk buckled himself in, and as I pulled the stairs up I heard the girl whimper, then felt a hand on my arm; the youngest of the men spoke quietly to me in Spanish, and Merk translated: the girl was sick, and needed to go outside. Merk yanked a plastic bag from the pocket on the back of the copilot's seat, but it was too late. "It's the worst part of the trip for them," he said. "The rest, they won't know what's happening."

Reducing the load, saving weight, he had told me, was one of the reasons he had removed the seats from the cabin. Now I knew the other reason—all three men were sick shortly after take-off, and the girl couldn't seem to grasp the idea of what the plastic bags were for. The smell of vomit was overpowering, and it was all I could do not to join the party. We left the airfield and dropped into a void, into a canyon, the walls of which were visible as a shade blacker than the horizon— the end of the strip was the end of the mesa, and we fell in a long, sagging arc to pick up speed, then climbed slowly, the stall-warning buzzer like a rattlesnake at my feet. Merk told me to keep an eye on the horizon; the horizon was the key to flying low, sometimes the only way to determine where the ground ended and the sky began—and I reached around the back of the seat, dragged one of his handy trash bags forward and stuck it between my legs, swallowing a surge of bile that had already reached my throat.

We headed east, gradually descending toward the high desert plateau. Two of the men sat cross-legged with their backs to the cabin walls; the others huddled between them, the girl curled up with her head on the younger man's lap. They spoke a language Merk didn't know, a Mayan dialect— *Quiché*, he thought—but the young man and the girl also spoke Spanish, and it was through the girl who eventually grew bold enough to sit up and peer out a window that I learned their names. She was Eugenia, and her brother was Cipriano; Luis was her father and Oliverio her uncle; her mother was Guadalupe and the baby was Maria Antonia. I prompted Merk, and Eugenia told him she was glad they had left the refugee camp because they had no home there, but she didn't like the ride north, three days in the back of a truck and two more on burros into the mountains. I asked about their homeland, why they had left, and it was Cipriano who said that they had been attacked by *guerrilleros*, that two of his brothers were dead. I had more questions, but Cipriano retreated into the darkness where I couldn't see his face, and now Merk seemed too obviously preoccupied with the task of flying, feigning interest in the various switches and gauges on the instrument panel.

We reached the city of Chihuahua in less than an hour, passed above the factories and warehouses on the southern edge, and made a long approach to the airport. But at the last minute, Merk pulled up and climbed out to the north, a move he said he hoped would confuse anyone tracking Mexican aircraft from the U.S.—one small plane had landed at the Chihuahua airport and another had taken off, routine flights probably, nothing to be concerned about.

At eight thousand he leveled off, heading directly for the border. There was little doubt we were now being monitored by U.S. radar, but we were high and in a groove, not trying to hide fifty feet above the desert floor. I passed the canteen around and everyone drank, including the baby, a tiny girl dressed in layers of crepe-paper-like clothes, a knit hat set low above her enormous black eyes.

Our approach to the *Aeropuerto International* in Juarez was slow and natural, running lights and strobes on, but with no radio communication. The city festered in smoke, and I could barely make out El Paso on the north side, the river hidden in a cloud of luminous haze. Eugenia, kneeling between the seats in the cockpit, watched as Merk turned from base leg and jockeyed into position for the tiny runway lights ahead, but when he lowered the gear he told her to sit between her parents in the cabin. We were on final to Juarez International, and for a second I had the wild and alarming thought that I had been set up, that I had been caught in a sting and this Merk character was actually a *Federale*, some sort of bizarre undercover *Aduana* cop.

"If they freak," Merk said, "do what you can to quiet them. Otherwise, stay buckled and keep your eyes open; let me know if you see anything." He flipped the landing lights on.

"Anything what?" I said. I saw plenty, and most of it was coming up fast.

"Towers, TV antennas, anything higher than us that's in the way."

There were no antennas, there was only the runway—
what was he talking about? But the instant the tires hit he
killed the landing lights and jammed the throttles forward,
killed the strobes also and tookoff again, banked left off the
field and shot into a neighborhood bristling with telephone
poles and TV aerials. Someone groaned behind me but I
couldn't turn to look—we were half-flaps and he hadn't
raised the gear and although I knew somewhere in the back of
my mind where we were going, I was also certain he wouldn't
try it, certain he'd turn east and head for the desert.

"What are they doing?" he shouted.

I glanced back. "Nothing. Praying, I think."

He nodded. "Chamizal," he said, pointing with his chin
out the window, and I caught a glimpse of the Cordova
Bridge, the Rio Grande as we hurtled into El Paso.

And through the downtown area, now above an empty
Interstate 10, the wing nearly level with the sign on the
National Bank building, a pair of smokestacks looming omi-
nously ahead. We cut right, skirted the Sun Bowl at the base
of Mount Franklin and settled in over the freeway again,
heading north, gear and flaps down, no lights, grinding out
an airspeed of ninety that felt like forty-five, passing the
occasional car but not by much. "Radar," he said, sitting
straight in the seat, straining to see over the instrument
panel. "They blanket the desert with radar, out east and west
of here and as much as two hundred miles into Mexico. In
my dad's day they used to have these mobile radar trucks

they'd stick in a likely spot. Now they got the balloons. Try to sneak across the border out there, they see you all the way."

"So you pretend you're *Aeromexico*, Chihuahua to Juarez."

"Right. A domestic flight."

To our left was the river and the state of New Mexico, the endless night west of El Paso. Below was Interstate 10 and a large gas station at an off-ramp, and unless I was mistaken, Merk had just pulled back the stick to hop over a bridge. Eugenia and her family lay in a dark mass on the cabin floor, still and silent.

"Then why the trapeze act over the freeway?" I said, feeling slightly detached, barely able to throw my voice out above the roar of the engines.

"Downlooking radar. AWACs, Orions, they can track us from above. Here we look like a truck, just another semi on the interstate."

I didn't doubt it. Because at the moment we were slowly gaining on a speeding Kenworth that had just passed a car.

"The people in the car, can't they see us?"

"Not unless they look up. And then we'd be a shadow, and they'd practically have to know what they're seeing. They can hear us, though. Last week I got chased by a cop, down on the freeway in a squad car trying to get my numbers with his spotlight."

"What did you do?"

"I outran him."

He smiled, but didn't move, didn't so much as blink. We

passed another truck. Tower lights above us on Mount Franklin flashed red, a warning to low-flying aircraft. A minute later the neighborhoods grew sparse, and I could see the glow of Las Cruces in the distance to the north.

"What about this military equipment they're using, night vision and all that? They see you, they'll call ahead and scramble helicopters in Albuquerque or wherever."

"They'd have to be waiting for me. Or like the cop, he'd have to sit out there listening with his window open, night after hot night. They don't have the manpower or the patience for that, and even if they heard me go by, they'd have a hell of a job scrambling something in time to find me."

"Yes, but suppose they get your numbers? Suppose they know who you are?"

"Well, that's a different story. They could bug the plane in my hangar, which I'm careful about, or my next trip they could watch me leave and figure I'm heading south. But even then, who's to say I'll use this route back? So they get all this expensive equipment in the air waiting for me, and a day or two later I show up in Albuquerque with a clean plane and a smirk on my face."

"Okay, but let's say they're on to us tonight. Say they're lucky and they picked us up coming across the border."

He shrugged. "They're in a helicopter, we're out of luck. In a Mohawk, I don't know—they can't land behind us with me in the middle of the strip. Years ago they'd follow by sight, get right on your tail and call ahead to all the local sheriffs where they thought maybe you'd land. Now they use lock-on devices and tail you from miles back. We'll do a little number above Las Cruces to see what's behind us, but the best way is to do like my dad did, put a couple of spotters on the ground along your route, give them night vision and portable FMs and have them radio you as you fly by, tell you what's following. But that's for dopers—I don't have the money for that kind of operation."

"So they might be tailing us right now."

He grinned. "They might."

"What then?"

"If we see them, we go back to Mexico where they won't follow."

"And if not?"

"What then is we go to jail." He tilted his head toward the rear. "And they go back to Guatemala."

Just south of Las Cruces he pulled up suddenly and banked right, brought the gear and flaps up, and put us into a tight 360 degree turn, then another, the two of us searching the murky light above the city for aircraft behind us. He made a pass on the Las Cruces airport, then switched the running lights on, and we climbed slowly in a wide spiral, higher and higher, Merk telling me we were legal now, but all the while checking for other planes in the sky behind us. Finally we headed northwest, toward the mountains, and Merk sat back, pulling on the front of his shirt as if to dry it.

"That freeway thing worked pretty well," he said. "Big-time smugglers have the equipment, the fast planes, all the updated info on customs—they can track whoever's tracking them and react accordingly. Me, I'm just a Juarez taxi, so I took the freeway."

"You say that past tense."

He looked at me. "You think you'd be here if this weren't my last trip?"

I didn't reply.

"Hey, don't sweat it. That cop with the spotlight told me my time was up. My old man had more than one trick in his bag, so I've got plenty of options." He paused. "Listen, there's always going to be folks who want to come here and always somebody to bring them, and no walls or fences or Border Patrol can stop it from happening. Today I'm a Juarez taxi, tomorrow I'm something else."

I was in school in the eighties when the boat people began arriving in Miami, the Haitians packed shoulder to shoulder in leaky skiffs, so many of them drowning in the surf and washing up on crowded beaches. I couldn't understand how anyone could be that desperate, risking death just for the chance to live out their lives in some urban hell like Liberty City or the South Bronx. But in San Antonio recently, in the basement of a "safe house" run by Peace Without Borders, I met a man from San Salvador who described the cardboard *colonia* where he had lived, a stinking, crowded sewer of a neighborhood at the edge of the city dump. He said it wasn't poverty or fear that sent his people north, it was that they had lost hope, and here in the states at least there was a chance, if not for them, then maybe for their children or their grandchildren.

"I thought we were going to Texas," I said.

"No, I don't land in Texas. I don't know much about Texas."

"So we land in New Mexico and somebody drives us to Texas?"

"That's right."

To San Antonio the long way, I thought. I said, "And where will they go from there?"

We were high and climbing through eleven thousand feet. Merk leveled out and handed me the controls, told me to aim for a tower beacon to the north, barely visible below the stars along the horizon. I had never flown a plane, but I had read enough to know that when trimmed and cruising they will practically fly themselves. I took the wheel in my fingertips, kept my feet flat on the floor and away from the pedals. Merk rubbed his neck and stretched his arms, turned finally and spoke to Cipriano in Spanish, then to me.

"They don't know. They have no people here, no money." He faced forward again. "It's usually this way. Sometimes there'll be a relative in L.A. or Miami, but mostly they're on their own."

"And yet they're lucky," I said.

"That's right. You ever see *El Corralon*?"

I hadn't, but it was on my list: it is an I.N.S detention center in south Texas—some call it a concentration camp—now with a big-top tent and a capacity for ten thousand. My plan was to travel with the refugees first, then finish with a trip along the U.S.-Mexican border, mostly as a guest of the Immigration and Naturalization Service. *El Corralon* would be my last stop. I told Merk all this, and he said:

"You're not going to take sides, right? You want to do it all and then write your book with no bias. These folks are being robbed and beaten every night along the border, half the women raped, and for those who make it across but get caught by immigration, the big reward is *El Corralon*. And you, you're going to finish this trip and then travel with the Border Patrol and tour the detention centers and get both sides of the story, and somehow through it all manage to remain in the middle."

"Like you, I'm in this for the money," I said, and immediately wished I hadn't—I'd meant it as a joke, but it didn't come out that way, maybe because he was right: I intended to ride the middle, all the way to the last page if I could, mostly because I figured I'd miss something if I took sides.

Merk shook his head. I was still flying this thing, this ancient "T-bone," and now he began a check of the instruments, tapping a reluctant gauge and scanning the panel with the flashlight, aiming it at the fuel switch on the floor and then back into the cabin behind us as if searching for leaks or cracks that might suddenly worsen. And as he did this it dawned on me that at this very moment I was risking my life, that while hanging over the freeway from El Paso to Las Cruces I had probably been closer to death than I wanted to be. And it also occurred to me that I was no longer along for the ride—by the simple act of steering this old bird toward God-only-knew what lay ahead, I was participating in that risk, and money, or even a book, seemed a weak and improbable motive.

The tower turned out to be an antenna on a mountain near the town of Magdalena, and as we approached, Merk took the controls and, easing the throttles back, began a slow turn to the west, pointing out the beacons atop the Very Large Array discs in the plain of San Augustin. A minute later he switched the radio on and adjusted the frequency, and descending rapidly now, we passed above a highway with a single car on it, and Merk leveled the wings, gave it partial flaps, and coaxed the throttles forward again. There were hills to the west, directly in front of us, and almost instinctively I checked for the horizon out my side window to the north, straining at the same time to see the ground. We passed a ranch house, and now ahead and to the south was another, lit up by a streetlight on a pole not far below us, and Merk, sitting straight and with his head nearly touching the ceiling, reached forward and grabbed the mike, clicked it twice, and twice again, then dropped it in his lap and lowered the gear. They appeared almost instantly: two faint strobes at the near end, and what looked to be automobile headlights at the far end, the strip no more than a few miles away. Eugenia had fallen asleep with her head partway between the front seats, and I motioned for Cipriano to hold her. The other men had stretched out on the floor, one on either side of the mother and baby, and had pulled the blanket nearly over their heads. Merk flipped the landing lights on, shoved the throttles forward, then yanked them back, tipping the wings into a crosswind, once, twice—then flared out for the landing. We floated past the strobes and settled onto the gravel strip, suddenly everything vibrating, Eugenia crying out as Merk cut the lights and braked hard, dust swirling up from the props and into the beams of the headlights now approaching us from in front.

I released the seat belt and started back. Luis and Cipriano sat up cautiously, glancing at the cabin windows. I stepped around them to the rear and pulled the latch, then pushed the door open. This time Merk had left the engines running, and in the blinding dust I nearly jumped into the path of the truck as it pulled next to the stairs. Seconds later a man wearing a headband, tall and wiry and who could have passed for Merk's brother, ran to the door and shouted up at me.

"You the gal writing a book?"

I nodded, and he pointed at Eugenia.

"Help me get 'em outta there. We ain't got all night."

I lifted Eugenia. Luis helped Guadalupe with the baby, while Cipriano and his uncle followed. In a minute they were out of the plane, Headband leading them to the rear of the truck. I jumped down . . . and saw Headband returning, an arm protecting his face from the stinging dust, his open ranch shirt flapping wildly in the prop blast. He grabbed my shoulder.

"Get 'em in the truck, will you! They won't listen to me."

"I don't speak Spanish," I said.

"Then pick 'em up and put 'em in, dammit! I ain't got time to teach 'em how to talk!" He turned to the plane just as Merk appeared at the door and handed him an envelope. I was certain there was money in it.

The pickup was an old seventies model, with no camper shell and the rear panel badly dented. The tailgate was down, and they were huddled behind it, their backs to the plane. I sat on the gate and swung my legs up, motioning for Guadalupe to do the same, reached for Eugenia as Cipriano hopped up beside me. In the bed near the cab I found a tarp. I unfolded it, told Cipriano with hand signals to keep the others down, below the sides of the bed and beneath the tarp. Headband had left the truck door open, and in the light from the cab through the rear window I could see their faces, all of them questioning me with their eyes, trusting me as if I were someone they knew.

I looked up. Headband was waving at me, gesturing frantically for me to climb in the cab so we could leave. I dropped over the side, and Merk appeared at the cabin door again, this time with my notebook in his hand—I had left it in the cockpit, and probably would have forgotten it if he hadn't brought it to me. I took it, and through the dust I thought I saw him smile his toothless smile, but just as I lifted my hand to wave, he pulled the door shut.

Headband ran around to the front of the truck, shouting as he went. By the time I reached the passenger's side he had slid behind the wheel and leaned across to open my door, but I hurried past it and to the rear gate, climbed over and into the bed. He watched me for a second, shrugged, then backed the truck away from the plane. Merk ran the engines up and began his roll, and in the noise and blowing sand, with the truck lurching to a stop and then leaping forward, I crawled under the tarp next to Cipriano, pulled it over my head and wondered why there were no mats on the steel floor, no blankets to keep us warm, no food or drink for our long trip to Texas.

Do I Know You?

Hank has rented a house. Mel, the woman he met on the ferry from Isla Mujeres and then traveled with for nearly a month, showed up in Crested Butte last week with her knapsack and a typewriter and asked if she could move in with him—because she needed a place to "create," as she put it. And of course his apartment with the tiny loft, as much as he loved that place, was just too small for the two of them, so he rented this house, a two-story affair built over and around an ancient log cabin, with plenty of odd little rooms added on, storerooms and sheds and even a downstairs bathroom that resembles the original outhouse but with plumbing. The rent is low because it's in town and not at the ski area, and there are three bedrooms upstairs, so Mel has her own room and even a den in which to write.

Mel, however, has made it clear: six months is all she can stay. She has it all planned out: twelve pages a week, two chapters a month—even the day she leaves (and the hour, 8 A.M.) is

noted in her journal, which she presented for Hank's inspec-
tion (along with her traveler's checks) as part of her pitch for
a room, telling him she was here to visit, yes, but she had to
write this book.

So it isn't what you would call a blossoming love affair,
even though it seems that way to everyone else, especially
since the story got out about them hitchhiking together in
Mexico this past summer—and now here she is in this out-
of-the-way Rocky Mountain town, moving in with a guy that
everyone knows is a consummate bachelor. And Mel is probably half his size. Very pretty but very short, five-one and
hardly a hundred pounds. Just the opposite of all the women
he has forever dated but never married, the tall and stately
blondes (and beautiful, as his sister is, and his mother was,
even until her last day), which alone raises the proverbial
eyebrow in this sometimes gossipy little town. His ski patrol
buddies, jocks all of them, go out of their way to heckle him,
come to the restaurant and sit at the quiet end of the bar
where no one ever sits. "Is the big dude hanging up the skis?"
"Hey, when's the wedding, Hopalong?" (God, he hates that
name!—to be a Texan in Colorado is to be relentlessly
cursed as a flatlander and a cowboy; he should never have
put spurs on his ski boots that first year—it was a joke!) And
of course Jarrold, his boss, is already worried about having
to find a new bartender, and Jarrold's wife, Toni, now eyes
him as though he's a deserter. It was obvious Toni didn't like
Mel the instant she saw her. When Mel arrived Hank took

her to the ski area to show her where he works and no
sooner are they in the restaurant than Toni is glaring at her,
and Mel says, "What are *you* looking at!" To the boss's wife!
Needless to say, he and Mel didn't stay long, and he found
someone to fill in for him for a couple of days after that, at
least until he could finish moving into the new house. And
then when all the heavy lifting was done and he was back at
work, his so-called friends started coming around with their
sneers and wisecracks, wanting the word on the "midget."
Mel hasn't got to them yet, but Hank knows she will.

Mel is a writer. She has had a book published about the
homeless, and when they met in Mexico she was near the end
of a trip to Central America, taking notes for another. A
month they had shared the road, and by the time they parted,
Hank had tried everything to convince her they should stick
together, they could work together or travel more together or
she could stay at his place in the mountains. But Mel had
said no, she needed to be in New York and then San Antonio
and she didn't know when she could get free, but she'd see
him again, she might show up in Crested Butte and surprise
him someday, she just didn't know when. That was the end,
Hank figured; he was certain he'd never see her again. He
couldn't say why he was attracted to her. She was strange and
she was tough, she was straightforward, yes, but to the point
of being dangerous to herself, and she certainly hadn't
shown much interest in him. It was odd how after she left he
couldn't stop thinking about her, remembering practically

everything she had said and done. And here he knew almost nothing about her, except that her only family is a brother in Omaha, and of course he related to that because now that his mother is gone, all he has is his sister . . . and all through Mexico Mel would mention these psychic powers she had, then quickly deny them or make a joke of them, but Hank saw her perform some uncanny tricks, if that's what they were, such as predict which cars or trucks would stop for them on the highway; she could read people's halos and auras also, and like a bird attuned to an impending storm, she could sense when things were about to change, and usually they would. Which, added up, led Hank to the idea that Mel somehow lived for the future, or even in the future. And there is this: Mel is very much present (or is it her sometimes overwhelming presence? Mel too often says what she feels), and yet, for him, she is so thoroughly absent: she plans her tomorrows as though dissatisfied with today, fending off the least bit of emotional contact from him by constantly rescheduling herself. To him she is here and she isn't here, or here and yet already gone . . . and it has occurred to him that this town is a curious place for her to have come to: Last summer in Mexico when she asked where he lived and he told her Crested Butte, she said she didn't like the mountains, she couldn't think in the rarefied air; for her the wilderness was no place to plan a future.

At any rate, this is Mel according to Hank, and Hank is not sure what he would hear if it were Mel according to Mel, although he imagines it as something intended: Mel two weeks from now, Mel as a goal she'd be certain to reach.

Thus with Mel showing up and the two of them moving into the new place and the changed atmosphere at work, it was a busy week for Hank. So that when Scott and his sister arrived on Saturday, Hank was tired and unprepared—although he knew probably better than most, especially after traveling with Mel in Mexico, that there are certain people and plenty of events you can never really prepare for.

Friday afternoon Scott had left for Denver, but not before he'd stopped by the restaurant for coffee and to tell Hank where he was going and why. Scott is a friend who is unlike Hank's other friends, not only because he is confined to a wheelchair but because he is self-reliant and responsible and acts as though he has already defeated most of life's ills. He is a newcomer to Crested Butte, having hired on last winter as a lift operator during the season; he drives his own specially built van and rents a room in a condo at the base of the mountain. He told Hank he was heading east to pick up his sister, who was a resident at a nursing home in Denver, and from there he would drive her back west to Grand Junction to visit their family, their parents and siblings in the town where they grew up. He did this every year, the last week in August.

But on Saturday when Scott detoured and stopped in Crested Butte on the return trip and came by the house shortly after noon—just as Hank was retrieving the news-paper from the front steps—naturally Hank was surprised because he had thought Scott would be gone a week.

Scott parked the van and cut the engine. His sister sat on the passenger's side, and never moved or turned her head. Her hair was pixie short, similar to Mel's, and Hank's first impression was that she resembled Mel, although she was obviously younger, close to Scott's age at twenty-two. Scott waved and then lifted himself toward the rear where he stored his wheelchair, and as Hank approached he caught a good profile of her face—pale and angular as if sculpted, oddly child-like and utterly still.

Scott opened the side door and called her name—Janice—by way of introducing her, and when Hank stepped forward she turned and looked at him with the strangest eyes he had ever seen, so vacant and yet penetrating, not dark brown or light brown but a royal brown, and as he drew closer he could see a faint scar across her forehead and another on the bridge of her nose, scars that seemed natural, that somehow gave strength to the frail beauty of that face.

But she was thin, wearing a flower-print dress that was obviously a size too large. She blinked and said, "Do I know you?", and the question stopped him: he had no answer to the odd inflection in her voice. And then Scott called him to the rear of the van and said she was amnestic—there was brain damage, a car accident when she was fifteen, damage that had destroyed her short-term memory—she could remember some of her past before the accident but nothing since; of the present she could retain nothing, no events, sights, smells—nothing beyond a few minutes of what for her was an eternal now. "Global anterograde amnesia," Scott called it.

She stepped out, and as Hank turned he saw Mel at the front door, and you might say that Mel and Janice locked eyes because they stared at each other for the longest time, all the while he pushed Scott in the wheelchair across the lawn. At first he thought Mel was angry, or maybe that she recognized this girl and was shocked by the sight of her, so serious was her expression. But then finally she smiled, and when Janice turned and looked up and down the street, obviously confused, Mel hurried toward her.

And this is when it began, Janice mimicking her, Janice becoming Mel. Arm in arm they walked to the house, Janice skipping once to match steps, then studying Mel's face, her eyes growing narrow and more focused, her lips full and more relaxed, like Mel's, tossing her head and swaying her hips as Mel does—until as they reached the door Janice had miraculously assumed the entirety of Mel's facial and bodily expressions; she was slightly taller and much thinner, but even her figure became Mel's—to Hank's amazement, her breasts seemed to grow in front of his eyes!

And Mel seemed amused by this, as though she'd expected it. In the house Scott explained that Janice would attach herself to certain women when she felt "lost," as she usually felt when not in the familiar environment of the home in Denver. "Janice mimics others because she has no self," Scott told Hank, and Janice followed Mel in from the hall, smiled at Hank with Mel's smile, and tilted her head in a coy nod. "Do I know you?" she said.

This went on for an hour, and although Hank tried, he couldn't adjust—he couldn't get used to the idea that Janice was so empty, that she had, in a sense, filled herself with Mel just to "be." And yet no one else seemed disturbed by this, not Mel or Scott, and certainly not Janice. Janice knew who Scott was whenever she turned his way, but with the sort of punctuated recognition of one who is surprised to see an old friend. Every time Hank left the room for more than a minute, when he returned he had to reintroduce himself or somehow answer the question "Do I know you?" But not Mel. Mel could leave and return and Janice seemed not to miss her, as though Mel had never left, and in an odd sense, she hadn't.

For Hank, feeling sorry for Janice seemed inadequate—he felt more helpless than sorry. He tried to imagine what it was like for her to be stuck in the present, to have as a reality whatever she could make up, whoever she could safely mimic. Scott said it was like continually waking from a dream and not knowing where you were. Yesterday for Janice was when she was fifteen ("she remembers nothing about the accident, or up to six months before it"), and yet she knew she had brain damage and knew she had trouble remembering things and somehow realized she was aging in a vacuum but couldn't understand why because she couldn't remember why. And the more Hank considered this, the worse he felt: she was so tragic, so hopelessly dependent.

But then a strange thing happened. She hung on Mel, mimicking Mel's voice, Mel's gestures, everything. And for a long time Mel put up with this, accepted this as natural, as though Janice were a younger sister or even a twin. But then Mel began to withdraw, slowly at first, and then growing more and more quiet, folding into herself and glancing uncomfortably around the room . . . and it occurred to Hank that Mel had begun to see herself in Janice, and moreover, to see herself at the instant she was being herself—not in the future, not Mel becoming Mel, but Mel *as* Mel. And Janice, faced with a diminishing Mel, not about to let go of her new "self," began to take the lead in this bizarre relationship, as if she were Mel and Mel were Janice.

Hank and Mel were at the kitchen table with Janice, and Scott had lifted himself onto the couch in the living room. Janice was sipping tea, and abruptly she reached across the table and caressed Hank's face with her left hand and Mel's with her right. "I love this," she said, in a voice lower and softer than Mel's. "It'll be perfect. The three of us, we'll be so happy and complete." She turned to Hank, and the look in her eyes was unmistakable.

And not only was it clear that Janice wanted to make love to him, what was crazy was that suddenly he wanted to make love to her, knowing she was Mel, and even more incredible, that Mel might also want to make love (all the time they had spent together in Mexico, the week in this house also, and he and Mel had never even kissed; not that he didn't try, trying was the reason he'd approached her in the first place: when they met in Mexico she said, yes, they could travel together, but the last thing she wanted was another guy hitting on her, and if that's what he had in mind, forget it!).

Hank sat back in his chair and said to Janice, "Hey look, I'm just a regular guy,"—and couldn't believe he'd said that. He felt Mel catch her breath. She held it for the longest time, red-faced, until finally she laughed . . . which had the effect of popping a balloon in Janice's face.

Janice said, pouting, "Why can't we?" And Hank couldn't respond. What was the answer?—that love requires a history? That we can't because there's a wall between now and your past? What would that say to Mel?—he and Mel had the history, but she was never here for love; she was forever ten steps into the future, continually building her own wall. And Janice was saying, Let's make love now, with no baggage from the past and no thoughts of tomorrow. Which is exactly the way he wanted Mel, more times than he could count.

Mel said, "You can't, that's all."

"But he wants to, I can tell," Janice said, slumping in her chair and suddenly becoming Janice again, thin and frail. And Hank thought: No . . . making love to her now, to Janice as Janice, was impossible. I should leave the room, he thought. A minute, two minutes, she'll erase me. Do I know you?, she'll say.

Instead, he reached across the table. "There are other ways to touch," he said.

She pulled her hand away. "No there aren't." She glared at Mel. "Not unless you stop, right now. Not unless you stay here with me."

Mel looked at him then, and as fantastic as this seemed— for a moment, for one of those vertical slices of eternity, Mel lost it. She quit being Mel with a plan, Mel with the synopsis of the universe in her head—she sat rigid in her chair, a look of frightened amazement on her face, and then began inspecting her hands on the table, turning them as if unsure they were hers. Finally she took a breath and shivered, and with that gesture somehow passed the message on to Hank . . . and a real and physical message it was, a tingling sensation that began in his spine and spread upward across the back of his head and then, so deftly, so precisely, like the time-lapse opening of a delicate flower, peeled back the top of his skull and escaped, taking with it everything he had ever thought was his, was him. Exhilarated and terrified, he was gone, he was no longer himself—and yet he was here in a much larger sense, so that he too was Janice, with a past that no longer mattered, adrift in an unmitigated present.

It didn't last, of course—any longer, he knew he'd be a candidate for the state hospital. Janice saw Scott on the couch, and when she walked to the living room Scott sat up and grinned at her as if to say, You've been at it again, haven't you! Mel had recovered and had snatched her journal from the kitchen counter and begun writing furiously—probably material for her book, Hank thought, a chapter she had already completed at some future date.

Which is to say that everything returned to normal, quickly and completely, as though their combined consciousness were an enormous rubber band that had stretched and snapped back. Mel went upstairs with her journal and Hank began digging in the refrigerator—for what, he wasn't sure—still in shock, really, certain only that he'd never understand what had happened at the table.

Janice picked up a magazine, one of many that Hank had brought from his apartment and had left in a pile on the living room floor. She sat next to Scott on the couch and began flipping pages, and this time when Hank entered the room he announced his name. She nodded politely, and when he asked if they would stay for lunch, she dropped the magazine and bounced up with an enthusiastic "Yes!"

And what was different was that when Mel came downstairs to join them, Janice acted as though she didn't know her, and even seemed shy of Mel—maybe because the first thing Mel did after walking into the kitchen was touch Hank's arm, lightly, her fingers lingering there for a moment as she passed. It was, he thought, a sign to Janice, a warning not to mimic, not to become someone else. And Janice didn't—she placed herself at the kitchen table next to Scott's wheelchair and slowly, carefully, examined her sandwich, lifted the bread and poked at the ham with a fork, now and then glancing at Mel and at Hank as though they were strangers.

And Hank couldn't help seeing this as their loss, Mel's and his, although he knew they could never repeat the scene in the kitchen. But Mel had been so open to Janice—she had let Janice in, and she could have learned something from Janice. And now once again Mel had erected her wall, closing herself off by warning Janice to keep her distance. This was the Mel he knew, the Mel he supposed he'd always know.

Janice finished at the table and returned to the living room, there to begin anew the magazine she had already read. Mel moved the dishes to the sink while Hank and Scott split a beer and discussed the football team at Western State; Scott is a senior there, and an avid fan. Out of the corner of his eye Hank could see Janice on the couch, bent over the magazine in her lap, studying it as she had studied her sandwich, entranced. It was this she was allowed, he knew. This was her everlasting moment—a magazine, a plate of food, objects she could pour herself into with all the intensity of her empty mind.

And so it was over. Whatever had happened earlier had gone the way of Janice's memory. Now the entire event seemed remote, a mistake perhaps, something that had never occurred. Scott announced that he thought he should get back on the road for Grand Junction, and outside as he wheeled himself toward the van, Hank wanted to ask him if he was okay, if he needed someone to ride along or even to drive him to Grand Junction—Hank had no basis for this, and the last thing he wanted was to insult Scott, but he had a feeling that something was wrong, that something didn't jibe. Mel brought Janice out and ushered her to the passenger's seat up front. She closed the door and smiled at Janice, then turned to Scott and said, "You're not brother and sister, are you."

And Scott turned away, reached for the handle on the side door and held it for a moment, then slid the door back. "I was sixteen," he said. "We were coming home from a school dance and her parents were with us because they were chaperons. I must have taken my eyes off the road."

"Her parents were killed," Mel said.

Scott looked at Mel, then up at Hank. "Janice was my girl." He smiled weakly. "She still is."

And of all the surprises Mel had sprung—the wild predictions in Mexico, the auras and halos, showing up in Crested Butte, and now the knowledge of Scott and Janice—none meant as much to him as what she did next.

They watched Scott and Janice leave, then stood in front of the house for a long time, just the two of them on that empty street, Hank with his arms folded and Mel with her hands in her pockets. The view, as always, was postcard clear—from this edge of town, in practically every direction there are mountains, some as high and as rugged as the Rockies get.

And Hank knew that this is what held them there—the mountains. Not thoughts of Scott and Janice or what had happened in the house—but a horizon as clean and dazzling as polished crystal, luminous in the midday sun. Mel turned finally, and asked if someday he would take her there; they could hike from town, and camp at night, take nothing but their sleeping bags.

And then she lifted her hands from her pockets and held them in front of her and made a sort of triangle, as steep as the roof of the church on the corner, tapping her fingers together. When she reached for his hand he must have had a silly look on his face because she gave a little laugh, a sigh, and it occurred to him that he had never heard her laugh that way before.

Passing Through

J arrold is driving a rented Lincoln, brand new but already a hubcap is missing—probably stolen from the parking lot at the hotel in Philadelphia where he has stayed the past few days. Jarrold recalls his first car, a '53 Plymouth ex-taxi with holes in the roof where the light used to be, how he drove it right here along Long Beach Boulevard on warm summer nights and sometimes girls in their white shorts would wave at him as he floated by. But that was long ago, in the fifties when he was a teenager and worked summer vacations on a fishing boat under the scorching sun all day, spent his nights in an overturned sailboat in the dockyard slapping mosquitoes and wishing the cabin ceiling weren't so hard. Oh that old Plymouth was his salvation, "nosed" and "decked" and "primered," so silly it was cool; in the evenings he'd drive the length of the island from Barnegat lighthouse to Beach Haven picking up pals and hitchhikers heading for the movies or maybe going nowhere at all, and then, as if he really were a taxi, drive them back when the show was over, the night a shade darker than he wished and the ocean breeze turning chilly.

Red, she called him. Reddy, Because of the auburn in his slicked-back hair. Her name was Audrey and, like Jarrold, she was from Philly; she called him Reddy one night in front of his buddies at the Dairy Queen where she worked and he took that name the way he took a good tan in the sun.

So he quit the fishing job and moved into a hollowed-out redwood log that used to be a gift shop on the main drag in downtown Beach Haven, with twenty cots in it supposedly only for lifeguards, twenty-five cents a night. Audrey lived with her mother in a cottage in Beach Haven Terrace two miles away, and this was as close as Jarrold could get, too close as far as Audrey's mother was concerned, but he'd meet Audrey every day and sometimes they'd walk along the beach near the water where the sand was hard; once, that first time, on a hot afternoon in August, they swam a quarter mile out with the lifeguard blowing his whistle and everyone on the shore watching, far beyond the surf so no one would see them kiss.

And now in his rented Lincoln, on a mild November day all these years later, Jarrold has come south on the same boulevard, down the spine of this narrow island on the Jersey coast—through Ship Bottom, Brant Beach, Beach Haven Crest, past a changed Beach Haven Terrace and finally into the town of Beach Haven. There are buildings he doesn't remember—the motel complex on the beach looks to him as though it had floated here from Atlantic City, and the diner where he used to hang out is gone, and so is the screened-in clam bar that for years served the best cherrystones in the world. But the old three-story rooming houses are still around, big complicated affairs with wraparound porches, some with elaborate outside staircases three and four levels high, shiny white against the chocolate-colored shingles. On a wide avenue a block from the ocean Jarrold stops in front of an anchor-shaped sign attached to one of these splendid buildings: "Rooms," it says, "Welcome," and Jarrold considers staying the night, finishing his trip to New York in the morning. But then an elderly gent wearing a captain's hat appears at the screen door; he sports a white beard and dark glasses, behind which Jarrold imagines a pair of sea-blue eyes now landlocked and slowly drying in bowls of crusty wrinkles. The man tips his hat and opens the door, but Jarrold drives away, turns left, and heads north along the beach road.

Jarrold has come here alone. He has forced himself to take this vacation. Two years ago, reeling from a divorce, Jarrold quit his job as vice president of Penn Chemical in Philadelphia, moved to Colorado, and married a younger woman. Now he lives in a picturesque Rocky Mountain town where he and his wife Toni own a restaurant at a nearby ski area. Except Toni is pregnant. Bad enough that Jarrold is middle-aged and unprepared for fatherhood, far worse that Toni has recently admitted the child is not his—this pregnancy is the result of a one-night stand, Toni having met an old lover named Dwight in a hotel near the restaurant, early one morning while Jarrold slept at home. And so Jarrold has come here alone, passing through, wondering when, or even if, he should return. He has visited old friends in Philadelphia, returned to U. Penn, his alma mater, and even to Germantown Academy, the school he attended in the neighborhood where he grew up. From there he had planned to cross the Delaware and catch the Jersey Turnpike to New York, turn the car in and then lose himself in the city, try to forget.

But instead he found himself at the cemetery in Haddenfield where his mother is buried, and from there, shuttled as if on automatic pilot out Route 70 past Red Lion to 72, down the old shore road to Manahawkin and across the causeway to Ship Bottom where, during the forties, his father had kept a beach house and where Jarrold as a kid— oh how clearly he remembers!—had once hid in a shed Labor Day weekend so he wouldn't have to return to the city and to school. His father sold the place in '48, Penn Chemical having suffered a mysterious loss, and thereafter Jarrold had to spend his summers at home in Philadelphia, eight long years in the city until he was old enough to drive his own car.

The way it happened, they said it was his fault. Her mother, even his buddies, said he knew she couldn't swim that well, and what was he trying to prove anyway, out halfway to the fishery nets? The police arrested him and held him until she was found, but no charges were filed. And then he couldn't attend the funeral, not because of her mother but because he was too stunned, too confused, shattered by a feeling that only years later he would know as grief.

What happened was this: they had been "going together" most of the month of August. They were a number, and everyone knew it. She was as tall as Jarrold, nearly five-ten, and she had green, opalescent eyes that when she leveled them at his would melt his soul; sometimes as they were cruising the boulevard she would stare at him while he pretended to concentrate on the road, and when he couldn't take it any longer he'd look at her and she'd smile, toss her long sun-bleached hair to one side and kiss his neck, kiss his arm all the way from his shoulder to his fingers on the steering wheel.

And they'd park at the beach, walk north away from the lifeguard chair, wade out to the sandbar, and at times it was so shallow you could kneel fifty yards offshore and the waves would hardly reach your chest. But the sea would pull them beyond, and it was there in the deep that one day Jarrold fell in love while she held him and kissed him furiously and surrendered as though shedding gravity itself. Every afternoon, out they'd go, farther and farther, each day reaching and then passing the limits of their love.

In Haven Beach Jarrold decides to return to the boulevard to get his bearings: there are new houses here, and probably more new houses to the north, and Jarrold isn't sure he will remember the street. But a block from the tavern in Beach Haven Terrace where he turns, he realizes he was wrong: he couldn't have missed it, not from any angle: it is a street that has hardly changed, a row of boxy Cape Cods with sand-tiled roofs, washed gravel lawns out front. And at the inter-section of the beach road again, second on the right, he sees it—the shutters are blue now, and the flower boxes are gone—but it is the same cottage, nearly fifty years old and looking new in its fresh white paint.

Jarrold pulls onto the beach road and parks. Somewhere a dog barks, a familiar sound. He knows if he turns and looks over the seat he will see the cottage through the rear window. It amazes him how clearly he holds the image in his mind: she stands barefoot on her front steps brushing her hair, her long brown legs shiny with oil, white white bathing suit bril-liant in the midday glare—he watches her in the rearview mirror as she casually turns the corner where he waits for her. As if her mother wouldn't know.

And under a cloudless sky in a glassy sea, with the sun hot on his neck as he swam ahead of her, stroking lazily for shore . . . she disappeared forever. She drowned without a cry, and the police finally had to put him in jail not because they thought he was guilty but simply to keep him from swimming back out there to find her.

His friends came to see him, but he couldn't answer their

questions. The cops told him three days later that she had finally washed ashore, his Audrey, so far gone they had to hide her body by covering it with sand until the ambulance arrived. And Jarrold left the jail that night and drove his ex-taxi across the causeway and as far inland as he could, away from the sea, away from the sand and the salt air and the morning sun, until he ran out of gas and had to walk to Philadelphia.

The beach is empty. Jarrold kicks off his loafers and starts across the sand, then stops and peels his socks down, rolls his pants halfway to his knees. The sand is cool and his feet are soft, the beach narrower than he remembers. He walks north, away from the toppled lifeguard stand. The sea is calm and nearly waveless. Past the jetty there are a few people, a man jogging at the waterline, lovers in the sand near the base of a dune. He walks on. Here, there is a shelf a foot high behind the tidal line, evidence of a passing storm, and the beach is scalloped in places, flat in others, as though gouged by a violent swash and then slowly repaired by a gentle but persistent breeze. There is driftwood in the wrack line, rockweed and sea lettuce, bits of whelk and cockle, a plastic bottle. Sandpipers scurry away as he approaches, and a tern dives at something offshore, changes its mind, and casually flies away.

Suddenly Jarrold stops and looks back, then turns again to the north. It was here—the fishery boats on their log rollers are gone now, but the pilings a mile out are still there. And as surely as he knows he has arrived, he also knows *why* he has come here, and yet the thought, the reason, escapes him. A gentle wave, larger than the rest, tumbles in and spreads itself in a wide arc, the icy water shocking his ankles. The backwash tugs at him, but his feet sink in the sand, and he thinks of the old man at the rooming house. He starts in, hesitates, then continues. He is knee-high in the freezing surf, his wallet, his pants and shirt already soaked, and a moment later he is past the breakers and into the deep. The water quickly numbs him, lulls him onto his back where he floats nearly submerged. He tries to imagine what it must be like to drown. The sun pulls at his face, but he hears and feels only the colossal silence of the sea, and slowly, with his body rocking in the gentle waves, he is filled with an overwhelming sense of freedom, as if in this return he had passed through an invisible gate she had all this time left open.

Orphan Ranch

There are animals everywhere. Poor Harry, Toni thinks. This is not the picture of her father-in-law she has carried in her head, not the way Jarrold described him, at least. Seven dogs and ten cats. How does he manage with this ragged crew? "Refugees from the animal wars in the county," Harry says, though Toni suspects he has been to the pound for most of them.

Of this hunch, for which Harry has provided names, there are two that Toni can stand: Rocko, head mutt and mediator between people and dog affairs; and Frank the Fireman, fastest cat in the west, always first to answer a food alarm. But there are also two she can do without: Snag, part German shepherd and part barracuda, who yesterday bit his way into a can of hash; and a paranoid cat called Loreta, a spooky black ghost living half-wild in the woods who occasionally appears at her bedroom window late at night to unnerve her. The rest of the four-legged mob is, as far as Toni is concerned, somewhere in the middle, but Harry worries about them all, especially when they put on their great act of shivering at the door for an extra handout. Even so, he enforces his one hard rule on the ranch: no animals inside the cabin.

Toni is into her eighth month of pregnancy, and she has come here to "nest," as she told Harry. When Jarrold left, she stayed in their empty house in Crested Butte for nearly two weeks and did her best to run the restaurant she and Jarrold own, but finally the loneliness got to her. That, and she didn't want Dwight coming back and finding her alone. So she placed Hank, their bartender, in charge and packed a bag. She thought about staying at her mother's in Denver, but with her mother's drinking problem . . . she didn't want to visit the past, especially not now with the baby coming. So she has come here, partly because Harry invited her and partly because she has nowhere else to go, although her idea of a "nest" it isn't.

It is a four-room, ninety-year-old cabin on eighty acres of Colorado mountain, a cabin on which Harry has just spent months of hard labor, shaping it to fit his needs. "Home" to Harry is Philadelphia, in the ivy-covered house he grew up in next to the Quaker school in the quieter part of Germantown. But soon after his wife died he retired as CEO of Penn Chemical, sold the house, and moved out here. "Why not!" he told Toni one day when she asked him why he had come all the way to Colorado. "How else could I escape the worried faces at my door, the pats on the arm, the offers of cooked food? How else could I be alone?"

So he sold the mock-Tudor in Germantown and called Jarrold the next day, said he had bought a ranch sight-unseen not sixty miles from them on the western slope of the Rockies. No glass in the windows, no running water, no kitchen unless you consider a broken wood stove and a chopping block a kitchen. But there was electricity, and with the help of a handyman from a nearby ranch, it soon became the cabin of Harry's imagination—the floors are polished hardwood, the walls are seasoned pine, there are desks and overstuffed chairs in every room. Toni calls it his "study." It is too serious for her, too woody and neat.

There is, however, an outhouse. Indoor plumbing will come later when the water rights to the property are amended, or so Harry says. Actually there are two outhouses: an old one next to the chicken coop, still in use, and a fancy new one of raw pine, now under construction above the narrow hole the handyman had the forethought to dig before the winter freeze set in. It is nearly completed, this new outhouse; there are tiles to be nailed to the slanted roof, the seat must be bolted on, the door hung. The design, Toni tells him, is "early Ozark"—she claims it is the most interesting building on the ranch, to which Harry responds by grinning in either appreciation or exasperation, she can't tell which. What is wrong with this outhouse—other than what is wrong with all outhouses—is that it is too far from the cabin, at least a hundred feet south of the rear door at the edge of a wooded area. To get there, one must hike the backyard, then execute a narrow plank across an irrigation ditch. Yesterday Toni declared it "scary" out there after dark, so Harry strung a long extension cord from the cabin to the trees, then fitted his new outhouse with a string of blinking, multicolored Christmas tree lights. Now, at night, and to Toni's delight, it flashes on the mountain like a hovel from outer space, just landed.

Today, she is on her way to the airport in Grand Junction, an hour's drive away. Yesterday Jarrold called from Philadelphia saying he had contacted Hank at the restaurant and found out she was here, that he was returning to Crested Butte and he wanted to talk, and anyway, he hadn't seen his father's new place yet. What he will say to her, she cannot guess. Last month when she finally told him the baby wasn't his, he left. For two days he moped around the house, refusing to touch her or talk to her, and then, from the porch, with his suitcase in hand, he asked how she knew it was Dwight's. But she knew; she had known all along, since the moment she walked out of Dwight's motel room the day after his visit, seven months before.

Dwight had called the restaurant and she had gone to his room to tell him to leave, it was different now. But he had talked her into it one last time, like every other time—he possessed this uncanny power over her, he had a way of making her feel indebted to him—and it was true, for the years they were together, she never loved him the way he loved her, and she felt she owed him for that, for all that had happened to him since. But there was also the risky sex, always taunting exposure, disaster—it was too familiar, and she knew it would never be that way with Jarrold.

And the disaster had come, the miracle within a miracle, despite her being on the pill. She was pregnant, and she couldn't bring herself to tell Jarrold. Dwight disappeared the way he had appeared, in a lie, and she was left with the truth and having to tell Jarrold. Abortion was out of the question. Jarrold was thrilled thinking the baby was his, and she was dying inside. One night, overwhelmed with guilt, sick at how weak she had been, she screamed and knocked the lamp off the bedstand, and Jarrold bolted upright in bed—it was the first time she had seen him afraid.

She understood that Jarrold had to clear his head, had to get away, but even then she knew he would go on wondering when it might happen again. She knew what Jarrold was thinking—that Dwight wasn't the only liar—and how could she say otherwise? Before Jarrold, her life with Dwight was a pendulum of promises and disappointment. She couldn't take it anymore; she came to the mountains; she wanted to start over. And then she met Jarrold when he moved in next door. He was perfect. Smooth, easygoing, prepared—in many ways just the opposite of her—and she admired him for his courage to leave after his divorce, to start over, in a town and in a business he knew little about. He hired her to manage his new restaurant. They got married. They became partners. They are still partners—but will he trust her now;

how can she assure him it is over with Dwight? She is certain of this: She will not allow the baby to represent her mistake, not in Jarrold's mind or hers; she will not let this child be Dwight's hold on their future.

Jarrold's plane is on time. He looks tired, older; his hair is unkempt and his face is swollen with sleep. He carries his suit bag in one hand and his down-filled jacket in the other and makes no attempt to put either down when he greets her with a "Hi."

Toni drives and Jarrold stares out the passenger's side window. They pass through Grand Junction and out east on Highway 50, toward Harry's ranch. Jarrold has not been here before; in fact, the last time he saw his father was at his mother's funeral when he and Toni flew to Philadelphia, last spring. Jarrold and Harry were cordial then, but little more. No hugs, certainly no tears; Harry insisted they stay at the house, but Jarrold checked into a hotel, claiming the old house held more memories than he could deal with. Jarrold was shocked when Harry, only a month later, quit Penn Chemical and moved to Colorado, of all places. Toni wonders how they will get along now, especially since Harry has, to use Harry's term, "blossomed" in his retirement. She wonders what Jarrold will think of Harry's new ranch. She wonders also what he will think of their Las Vegas outhouse.

She will find out soon enough: As she turns into the driveway there is a terrible commotion on the porch—animals clawing for traction, animals yapping into the yard and around the car. When she stops and cuts the engine and Jarrold steps out, he is immediately surrounded by dogs sniffing his shoes. Jarrold eyes them warily, then peers over his sunglasses at Toni as if to say, "This zoo was your idea, wasn't it!"

Inside, Jarrold drops his suitcase and shakes Harry's hand. Immediately he wants a tour through the cabin. He tells Harry it is straight from the pages of *Town and Country*, and when Harry says, "more like *Outdoor Life*," Jarrold shrugs and nods and follows him into the kitchen.

Harry has prepared a roast for dinner. While Toni was at the airport he even set the table, normally Toni's job since she has been here: Harry buys the food and cooks it; Toni sets the table and washes dishes. Harry has put Jarrold and her on the same side of the table, across from himself. He announces in one breath as he carries the roast from the oven that dinner is ready and that he has put the finishing touches on the outhouse, hung the door and added a padded seat he bought from a mail order house. Jarrold looks at him as if he were daft.

Dinner was excellent—Harry has outdone himself. He and Jarrold have finished their second brandy, and Toni has put away the last of the dishware. The talk at the table was mostly Harry about Harry: his departure from Penn Chemical, the move to Colorado, the refurbishing of the cabin. And then he wanted to hear about Jarrold and Toni's restaurant in Crested Butte, something he had not asked

Toni during her stay. Jarrold told him the whole story, from leasing the property and initial construction to hiring the staff and opening day, all the while glancing at Toni and including her, for which she was grateful.

It is late, and Harry announces that he is tired. Jarrold dons his jacket and declares he will attempt a trip to the outhouse. Harry offers to show the way, but Jarrold is certain he can find it—who could miss it? Harry tells him he will be the first to use the new outhouse, only fitting since he is the guest of honor for the evening.

Jarrold leaves by the back door. Harry winks at Toni and bets that this will be Jarrold's first experience with an outhouse. Snow has begun to fall. The temperature has dropped sharply in the last few hours. Toni catches herself picking her nails, while Harry peers out the kitchen window. Toni feels they are waiting for a scout to return from a dangerous mission, a point man sent off to reconnoiter an enemy stronghold.

Suddenly Harry gasps, and Toni looks up just in time to see the outhouse door bounce back on its hinges and slam shut, then waggle open again—and there is Jarrold, pants down around his knees, lurching into the snow from the blinking interior. He slips on the plank and falls partway into the ditch, and Toni is out the door, holding her belly and hurrying to him. "My God," she hears Harry say from the door, "it really was his first trip to an outhouse."

Jarrold struggles into the cabin. "There's a snake out there," he says. He is shaking. His eyes are enormous. A snake? Toni thinks. What snake would brave this weather, and if it did, wouldn't it be stiff, too cold to strike? "It b-bit me," Jarrold stammers, and he grabs Toni's hand and tows her to the bedroom.

Jarrold cannot see the wound in the mirror, so Toni inspects. It is not the sort of snakebite she expects, so she hands Jarrold a towel and tells him to wait. She is out the back door again, this time with a flashlight. Harry yells from the door that she is top-heavy, to be careful crossing the plank. In the outhouse she shines the flashlight in the hole and sees Loreta, the cat, staring up at her. Suddenly it leaps up and scrabbles at the edge of the seat with its front claws, until Toni grabs it by the neck and hooks it to her sweater. Toni carries it outside and across the plank, nearly to the cabin before it struggles free and scampers into the woods.

"That was the snake?" Harry asks at the door, and Toni has to clench her teeth to keep from laughing.

"She took shelter in the pit," Toni says. "She got scared when Jarrold sat down."

It is noon. Toni has spent the morning packing the few things she brought, moving furniture and replacing Harry's knickknacks in the spare room she has occupied this past month. At breakfast Harry told the story of how, when he was a kid, he and his best friend Corky O'Hara got into it over a missing baseball card—they were each certain the other had pilfered it from the scrapbook they shared. Just then the neighborhood bully, a fat brute named Newton, rode by on his bicycle. As it happened, Newton was so intent on watching them square off that he crashed where he had no reason to; he simply fell over and skidded down the sidewalk. This was so hilarious—Newton tangled in his twisted bike, Newton furiously struggling to his feet—that Corky O'Hara got sick from laughing too hard, laughing first at Newton, then at Harry laughing at Newton, then at the two of them laughing at each other. Eventually Newton came back and punched them silly for having fun at his expense, but the point is this: Newton's mildly amusing accident triggered in them a veritable geyser of suppressed feelings, a hooting, whooping, snorting fountain of week-old, pent-up emotion that made them forget why they hated each other; in fact, by the time Harry led Corky to the bathroom in his house, the idea that they had been angry for a week over a baseball card—that in itself was unfathomably funny.

Which is, of course, what happened with Jarrold and Toni: Jarrold's embarrassing moment in the outhouse was the crack in the dam, their laughter the wedge. In the bedroom again she told him about Loreta, and she couldn't help it, the memory of him lurching into the snow, the claw marks on his butt—she tried to keep from laughing but the snickers escaped, and then Jarrold smiled, and soon they were sitting on the bed and cracking up. And then Toni found herself crying, holding herself and saying how sorry she was—and she knew the rest would follow, with time.

And so it is noon. She and Jarrold are returning to Crested Butte. She misses Crested Butte; she loves her home, her job, she will learn to love Jarrold. Jarrold told Harry that their departure, this new beginning for them, was all his fault—it was Harry who wouldn't allow the animals in the cabin!

These animals! Toni is trying to pack the car and they are wiggling at her feet. There is already a cat on the front seat so she can't close the door, and now Snag is woofing as though demanding to know where she is going. Where is Loreta? Toni thinks—probably cowering in the outhouse again; Harry will have to coax her out once and for all.

Jarrold comes out of the cabin with his suitcase. Harry is behind him in the doorway. Now all of the dogs and several cats are in the car. Terrific, Toni thinks. Harry calls them, but the dogs only bark and wag their tails. He tells Toni he has an idea. It is beginning to snow again, tiny flakes, two, three at a time, that fall like dust to the frozen yard. Now Rocko sits behind the steering wheel, peering through the windshield, while Snag rides shotgun. Harry opens the cabin door and rattles a pan of dry pet food. Rocko's ears spring up, and immediately he jumps out of the car, with Frank the Fireman close behind, then Snag and a pair of sinfully ugly mutts named Venus and Adonis, followed by a trio of cats. They wedge themselves in front of the door, sniffing as though wondering what sort of trick this is. Finally Rocko accepts the invitation. He steps shyly inside, ears twitching, testing the air with his shiny black nose. He looks up at Harry as if to say, "Really?" and when Harry pats his head, Snag places a paw on the step and grins. It takes a while, but now they are all in the cabin, eyes wide, noses alert, inspecting this house of the strange old man who adopted them.

In the driveway again, Jarrold shakes Harry's hand and tells him he is expected for Thanksgiving dinner in Crested Butte. Toni hugs him, and when she thanks him he smiles and looks away—she wonders if he will be lonely when she is gone, or if he is glad he will finally have his peace.

Jarrold starts the engine, and Toni closes the passenger's door. Harry steps inside, then suddenly appears at the cabin door again. He waves and hurries around the side of the cabin and over the plank across the ditch. He'd better do this quickly, Toni thinks, or Snag will make a meal of the canned food in the kitchen. Harry enters the outhouse, and in a moment reappears holding a ball of black fur close to his chest. "Will you look at that," Jarrold says, as though Harry were holding a snake and not a cat. Harry stops and waves again as Jarrold heads out the driveway, and Jarrold waves back. Toni shivers and rolls up the window. The baby kicks.

State Hospital

"Took me a month to get down here," Monk said. "Hobblin' around in my cell, crawlin' down the tier to the shower, all that time they think I'm playin' 'em for drugs. Shit, they run out of aspirin, so what do they give me? Midol. Like I'm havin' my period or somethin'!"

I knew. I had spent weeks in my cell with a herniated disk after a fall off a ladder, every night trying to sleep sitting up with my head on the metal desk next to my bunk, ankles the size of cantaloupes with edema because I couldn't lie down. The guards thought I was faking.

"Finally I tells 'em, 'I don't want no damn Midol. I don't want no excuses. You get me down the state hospital or I'm soooin' ya.' And the next day, sure as hell, they pack me up and ship me here." Monk chuckled, and shot a look over at Marty Gold in the next bed. "Hey Mart, how long it take you?"

Marty stared straight ahead, toward me on the opposite side of the room but past me, into the wall and who knew

how far beyond? Marty had severe colitis. As part of a battery
of tests he had been probed with a sigmoidoscope only this
morning, and his dark eyes in his pale moon face were still
glassy and slow.

"Years," Marty said.

Monk stuck his chin out. "Hey Mart, c'mon now, it don't
take years to get down to the state hospital. Weeks maybe,
months, but not no years. You ain't foolin' old Monk."

"I had pain," Marty said. "And gas. I had gas for years."

This brought an explosion from Monk, more a cough than
a laugh, one earsplitting guffaw that made us all jump,
everyone but Al. Monk shook his head and tugged at his
nose, then reeled his heavy ankle chain up onto the bed,
shook his head some more. Finally he said:

"Did they fix it, Mart? They fix yer tooter? They put a new
whistle on your teapot, Mart?"

When nurse Camden came in for the morning vitals check,
she brought four new trainees: two females and two males,
and not the same four that had been following her most of
the week I had been here, but a new group. One of the
females was half pretty, a chesty blonde with popping blue
eyes and poodle-pink lips, barely out of high school, I
guessed, and nervous, hugging her clipboard to her over-
sized breasts and avoiding our stares, wary of us as they all
were. And who could blame them? This was forensic surgery,
an entire ward of the state hospital packed with convicts,

three, four to a room, every one of us, according to their training manual, desperados and thieves, perhaps rapists and murderers, brought in from the various prison facilities in the state. And how should they treat us? Carefully. And what were their duties this first week? Perform minor but personal tasks: check temperature and pulse, fetch hot water bottles and bedpans, check IVs and catheter bags, make sure our water containers were full. Monk loved it, the very idea of it; the look on his face as they entered the room was that of a child at a circus, floppy clowns shuffling in to warm the crowd.

But nurse Camden was no fun, in her fifties at least and with an air of having been around convicts long enough to believe she held a thankless job, long enough to know that if she gave an inch, we'd take a yard. There were four of us in the room, Marty and Monk to the left, Al Garcia and me to the right, and nurse Camden wasn't about to warm to a single one of us; she planted herself hands-on-hips in the center of the room, stood there in her bulging white uniform like a buddha in a laundry bag as the trainees fussed over Marty Gold, and by the time they got to Monk's bed Monk was grimacing and fluttering his eyelids in a ludicrous rendition of a man in pain, already reaching for the blonde with the conical tits.

"S'a damn shame," he gushed. "Man like me, lyin' here hurtin', least I could get is a shot of dope and a backrub." The blonde pulled up short at the foot of the bed, and Monk struggled to sit up, groaning. A male trainee quickly stepped forward and shoved a digital thermometer in his mouth. Monk had much to say to the blonde but suddenly he couldn't, and already nurse Camden and the others were drifting across the room to Al Garcia.

Poor Al, paralyzed from the chin down, shot trying to escape the county jail, he had been in the papers for weeks, big-time bank robber who never verbally threatened the tellers he robbed but instead passed violent notes of beautifully crafted script; the cops dubbed him the "calligraphy bandit." Now he could barely hold his head upright, and he still didn't talk much; about the only thing he'd said to me the entire week was that he was thirsty, and would I push his call button for a nurse? Once, though, in a rare demonstration of verbosity, before Marty or Monk arrived, he told me he couldn't even kill himself, that was the thing, couldn't get a blade to his wrists or even get his damn head in the toilet so he could drown himself, that's how bad it was. I wondered then if he was going to ask me to help, but as though reading my thoughts he hitched back his mouth in a sorrowful grin and told me that nobody, nobody he knew, was stupid enough to catch a murder beef for his sake; nobody wanted life in prison or even the death penalty for putting some vegetable out of its misery.

I got the digital thermometer from the girl with the radical chest. She had darting, fearful eyes though, like a salamander, and strangely puckered lips, as if she were about to whistle, and it occurred to me as she roughly inserted the plastic shield under my tongue that I was lucky I didn't have a mouth injury, and besides, a woman with breasts the size and shape of howitzer shells never did much for me.

"Hey Camden," Monk shouted from across the room, now that the male trainee had removed his thermometer. "Where's the doc? What's old Sort-of gonna do about my back?"

Nurse Camden turned, her owly mouth set in a permanent frown on her otherwise impassive face. The day I first saw her I knew immediately she went by the book, not only at work but in her car driving to work and probably at home before and after work. She said to Monk, "You're scheduled for a myelogram, Mr. Pulaski. This afternoon." She tapped the metal railing at the foot of my bed with her clipboard. "Ask Mr. Pitts, here. He'll tell you all about it."

Which was her idea of a joke, since she and the others in the room knew I didn't talk. I haven't talked since I was a kid, and although I was nine or ten, I hardly remember now what it was like when I did. Some who don't know me think I'm either faking or I'm too stupid to use words, but the fact is I can't talk—the words form in my head, I can think, I can write, but somehow there is no connection to my vocal chords, even though there is nothing physically wrong or missing. It happened in childhood—my dad beat me, I stopped talking—and that was it.

Monk sat up, wincing with pain and regarding me now with a look of suspicion. I too had been half-crippled with sciatica, every day begging aspirin or Tylenol from the guards at the medium-security facility where I was housed. Finally they had brought me here, where a different set of guards stripped me and searched me and handed me a hospital gown, cuffed my ankles, and led me to a bed. The nurses performed their standard tests and did their paperwork for a few days while I sweated and tried to sleep, and then they sent me downstairs for a myelogram. Two days later they shot me full of Demerol and wheeled me into the operating room. A laminectomy, fairly routine, the removal of a lumbar disk, but something had gone wrong, and now I had no feeling in my leg, from hip to toes on my left side. The surgeon who did it was Sortif. Dr. Idlefonso Sortif. The same shifty-eyed, foreign-speaking bone-sculptor who would do Monk. Monk never could get the name straight. "Hey, Sort-of," he'd say whenever the doc made his rounds. "When're ya gonna do my back? Let's get with it, Sort-of, I only got forty years to parole!"

I sent Monk an airplane. Over the years I had got good at writing notes and sailing them as paper airplanes. I had a design that was compact, a tight wedge resembling a Stealth fighter. It flew straight, and when it ran out of thrust, it dropped straight. On it I had written, "A myelogram is how they separate the men from the malingerers. They put you facedown on this table under an X-ray and stick a needle the size of a fishing pole in your spine, squirt dye in there, and take pictures. It takes an hour or so, and afterwards you've got to lie flat on your back with no pillow for a whole day so you don't croak from a killer headache."

Monk read it, glanced over at Marty and at Al, then looked at me. "Yeah?" he said. "And what was the operation like?"

I shrugged.

"They give you enough dope?"

I nodded.

Monk frowned at my splayed feet, the articulated wave of my body on the old, hand-cranked hospital bed. His cheeks were blotchy red, the color of high blood pressure or heavy drinking, and he had shiny black buttons for eyes, curious and quick, set deeply below the prominent shelf of his brow; his nose was the nose of a prize fighter, flat and wide, as was his mouth—he did, in fact, resemble an ape, hence the moniker, but about Monk there was also a lightness, a quality I associated with spontaneity.

"But you went in crippled and came out paralyzed," he said, gaping.

I shrugged again.

Marty sighed and looked longingly at the intercom on the wall between the beds. Monk waited, then threw an arm out and punched it for him, and when a nurse answered he told her Marty's four hours were up, and she oughta get down here with a shot. He turned back to me.

"Sort-of?" he said. "Is that what you mean? Sort-of?"

This ancient hospital. Opened as an insane asylum in a tiny brick house nearly a century ago and expanding in fifty years to military base proportions, a sprawling and dismal complex on a few thousand acres west of the city. The present architecture is that of most government buildings of the post World War II era—huge rectangles of pink or sand-colored stone and brick, unadorned and uninspired, similar to the metropolitan housing projects of the same era, the schools and factories that multiplied on the outskirts of the cities before suburbs were invented. But in the fifties and sixties, as drugs replaced restraint and as state and federal funds were directed elsewhere, entire sections of the hospital grew obsolete and were closed, the buildings stripped and eventually condemned. Now only a few buildings are in operation, the largest and most central of the compound, but still with plenty of dimly lit single-corridor wards, both locked and open, high- to minimum-security, and still the surgery ward for prisoners, the only place in the state a convict can get his nose put back straight or his appendix removed or, God help him, a vital organ repaired or replaced.

Marty Gold wore ankle cuffs, as I did. These were similar to handcuffs but with a longer connecting wire, so a man could walk but not run. Monk, down from a maximum-security facility, was chained to his bed, and even the wheels were removed so he couldn't tow it around. Al Garcia they left alone—he wore no shackles or chains, and every morning the trainees or sometimes even the janitor would lift poor Al to his wheelchair and strap him in for the day.

But the chain clamped to Monk's leg was thick and heavy, thirty feet long and noisy whenever Monk dragged it to the bathroom. "Sorry fellows," he'd say in the middle of the night, "Old Marley's got to go." And then returning he'd stop at the only window in the room and stand there for the longest time, his broad back and hunched shoulders framed by the unnatural glare of the spotlights in the courtyard outside. Before my operation I would go to the window also. I would hear vehicles below, and once I saw a delivery truck in a narrow alley four stories down. This was the only opening to the street—an asphalt ramp leading from the basement of our building and passing between the end of east wing and the beginning of south; the remainder of the view was a large and barren quadrangle, and except for the ramp, entirely enclosed by the walls of the inner and forgotten side of the hospital, a grim mirror effect of opposing barred windows and broken rain spouts, trails of rust like grimy tears coursing downward as much as twenty feet from the windowsills of the upper floors.

So I knew what Monk saw during those trips across the room at night. He couldn't have known any of us were awake in the dark, and yet he'd stand at the window and shake his head and say things like, "Will you look at this, Alex?" Or, "They call this a hospital, Mart, a place to get well." One night he said, "Al, I'd hate to be you. 'Cause this here's worse than prison. Prison's this big hole they drop you in, and slowly you get to climb out, all the while they're kickin' you back down. But this here's the end of the line, ol' buddy. A man could die here and not a single livin' soul would know he was gone."

The day Monk arrived he told me why he was in prison: He was an orphan, reform school before the army, and Vietnam, and then on and off in the joint after that, small-time stuff—car theft, burglary, gambling—until finally they slapped him with the "bitch," declared him a habitual criminal and sentenced him to life. He couldn't shake that, he said, the idea of it, being locked up all his life, and somehow he never could play by the rules; it seemed he screwed up even when he tried not to. So now he was in Max with too much time and too many disciplinary reports, and the thing was, now that his back was out, he couldn't protect himself, couldn't even work off the tension playing handball or lifting weights in the yard—what kind of crap was that?

But he also had an impatient side that bordered on cruelty. One day he asked Marty if he was Jewish, and when Marty answered yes, Monk wanted to know what a "Jew-boy" was doing in prison—Jews were too smart and too rich to be in prison—and when Marty looked away and mumbled something about a fire, Monk snapped his fingers and said he remembered the local TV coverage—about the gay couple, and one of them set fire to their condo in a jealous rage, nearly killed his lover. "Was that you, Mart? You set that fire under your boyfriend? You like your sausage cooked, Mart?"

So Monk pestered him about being a "fag" and a "fairy" and a "queer," and anyway, how come with a violent crime like that he only got six years when he, Monk, was down for life? But maybe the thing that bothered Monk the most was that Marty wouldn't answer him, also the way Marty never said anything to the doctor or the nurses about the lousy food and the dirty sheets and the lack of attention. It was true: if you didn't ask, you didn't receive, and more than once I had to pester the nurses for a change of sheets or a clean hospital gown or a trip to the shower down the hall; they were busy, they were understaffed, they were trained to be aloof and suspicious. And so Monk would ride Marty, and Marty wouldn't say a thing, and then Monk would get frustrated and ride him worse or just grunt and shake his head and sit quiet for a while tugging on his nose until somebody changed the subject. Once though, after a long pause, he said, "Mart, you ever consider that if you'd had the guts to ask for what you need, you wouldn'a had to light that fire?" And Marty turned beet red and his eyes filled with tears, but he never said a thing.

It was the myelogram that got to him. They took him that afternoon, and when they brought him back his face was as gray as the bed sheets, his eyes glazed and jaundiced as though he had been poisoned.

He was laid out, of course, no pillow, flat on his back so the dye wouldn't circulate. And just before the five o'clock meal, old Doc Sortif came in polishing his glasses and telling Monk that they had discovered a herniated disk in the lumbar region and they'd be operating the following day—a laminectomy—nothing major, but he'd definitely be off his feet for a few days, maybe a week, because they couldn't send him back to prison until he could walk; that was the rule. And Monk didn't say a word, no wisecracks, no "Sort-of" this and "Sort-of" that; he just lay there staring off toward the ceiling until finally the doc turned and walked out.

Monk wouldn't eat supper or breakfast, even though it was the blonde who brought the breakfast tray and who offered to help spoon it into his mouth. I flew him a Stealth, and Marty asked him what had happened, what had gone wrong, but he wouldn't respond—hardly a ripple of movement escaped him. Late in the night, though, before sunrise, I heard him sigh, and I opened my eyes to see him sliding off his bed carrying his chain, heading for the toilet, and as always he stopped at the window—only this time he didn't say anything; he only stood there, hunched over with the chain in his hand, as though he were in pain but just had to stand there anyway, had to look out at that dismal floodlit courtyard as though it contained all the light left in the world.

"I'm glad he's gone," Marty said the next morning after they wheeled Monk out on a gurney to the operating room. Marty had sat up for breakfast but then couldn't eat; his eyes were still watery but at least there was a blush of color in his pudgy cheeks. "He's like all the other assholes in prison, loud and opinionated. Big macho know-it-all."

I wrote, "You mad about the 'queer' thing, Mart?" and sailed it over.

He glared at me. "So what are you in for?" He pointed at

Al. "What about him? How do we know he's really a bank robber?"

Al slowly raised his head. Al with the towel—most of the day he wore a towel draped over his head so that if he tilted it forward you couldn't tell if he was awake or asleep, and as he had once said to me, he couldn't tell if we were either. Today the staff from the operating room had moved him from his bed to his wheelchair before leaving with Monk, and once again he had settled into the slumped, rubbery posture he'd be in all day until someone carried him back to bed. The only break in Al's routine was his afternoon trip downstairs to physical therapy, a roomful of booths with massage tables and a bunch of antiquated machinery with big dials and fat wires, and also the whirlpool room where they took Al for his daily bath and massage. They had started me on the physical therapy also, this week, in the mornings, though, because I went for heat treatment and not the whirlpool, cuffing me to a wheelchair even though I couldn't walk and sending me off with one or another aide or trainee to PT. A long trip it was, too, out past the double security doors of our ward and down the elevator to the first floor, then the length of the building along the front corridor, left down another dim corridor toward the rear of the hospital where the kitchen and storage areas were, into the therapy room at the corner of the building. I had related all this to Monk the day before his myelogram, saying that if he had to have the operation, at least he could look forward to this—

there was a terrific masseuse in PT, young and shapely and with long delicate fingers; it was she who would remove your gown and help you onto the table, apply the balm with her miraculous hands and then place you under a heat lamp or ultrasound where, if you had a vivid enough imagination, you could nearly feel content.

Not Al, though. Poor Al couldn't feel a thing from his neck down, and there were times I wondered about his neck up also. Now his eyes were at half-mast, pointed in the general direction of Marty's bed across the room, but with no anger in them.

I told Marty I was in for murder, which was true. I didn't say anything about Al, and neither did Al.

In prison you never get an answer. The best you hear from a guard is, "I'll check on it" or "Let me think about that"—which, I have heard, are phrases included in the training manual as suggestions for managing inmates—say "No" or "I don't know" to a convict and you might provoke a confrontation, or at least be obliged to answer when he asks, "Why not?"

Which is to say that I never got the story, what really happened. Sure, there were plenty of rumors—prisons, ghettos, wherever there is a lack of hope, there are rumors—and you learn to sort through them, one by one, sifting out the bits of truth according to what you know, what is and isn't probable, who and where it came from.

The state hospital does not own tomography equipment, and probably never will. So they shipped me out to one of the downtown private hospitals where they have a million-dollar CAT scan set up, and as a result it was determined that somehow during my operation my spinal cord had been "bruised," and the numbness would most likely disappear in a few months. And so there I was in this fancy new hospital with electric curtains and color TVs and decent food for nearly three days. And then when I got back to the state hospital, Monk and Marty and Al Garcia were gone, and no one on the staff would tell me why or where they were or what had happened. "We'll check on it," was the best I could get.

It had to have been Marty who helped him. I say this because a man one or two days out of a laminectomy just doesn't lean over and pick a lock on his ankle, not to mention stroll across the room and lift another man out of a wheelchair and place him on his bed. Then too, the day after I got back, they moved a guy into the room who had just arrived from the same medium-security joint Marty was from, and he said Marty had never got back there—he thought he was still here. So I figured Marty had been shipped off to Max pending an investigation, and now the thing was for him to keep his mouth shut, because if he did he'd probably beat it, and if he talked, well, like a lot of guys in prison, he'd be his own worst witness.

Al is probably still in the hospital. Where else would they keep him, paralyzed like that? He's likely in one of those padded security cells they reserve for "live ones," locked down and on limited rations for a month. Poor Al. But what does he care? In his better moments I picture him in his padded cell smiling or even chuckling to what's left of himself, remembering what Monk looked like sitting in that wheelchair back on the surgery ward, after the switch.

But which staff member made the mistake? Who was it that never realized it was Al in the bed and Monk in the wheelchair? Yes, it was true: the blonde with the pointy breasts was gone; she had mysteriously vanished from the ranks of nurse Camden's trainees, and the convicts on the ward I could talk to—the staff had finally got me out of bed and into one of those old folks' walkers for exercise, twice a day down the hall pushing that aluminum embarrassment and dragging my dead leg behind, still chained to my good one—they said they saw her wheeling somebody out with a towel over his head the morning Monk disappeared, then saw her return ten minutes later, only to leave with security shortly before noon; one guy said he knew Monk personally, and the girl was Monk's old lady from the streets, had to be, sure, he'd seen them together in the neighborhood two years ago before Monk took this fall; it was a setup; Monk set the whole thing up, even had his old lady get a job here so she could wheel him out.

Which was horseshit. Monk wouldn't have gone through with the operation, not after a myelogram that had turned him green. What happened happened on a Friday, janitors in, showers going, doctors on their rounds, and in the confusion, the blonde never bothered to check just who was in the wheelchair with the towel over his head. And then also, for how many months, how many times had the nurses in the hall, the guards at the door, seen poor Al with that towel over his head, being escorted by one or another trainee to physical therapy?

So she had wheeled him out the security doors and off the ward, down the elevator, and along the corridors to PT at the rear of the wing, probably left him there in the foyer thinking he was poor Al, paralyzed from the neck down, no cuffs or chains on his ankles but no need to worry about him either, no way he could run or even wheel himself out.

And from there I could only imagine; from there the rumors flew in all directions; no line of thought, no bit of information was more logical than the rest. Maybe the therapist discovered him and called security. Maybe he was caught wheeling himself back along the corridor, searching for a way out or a place to hide. Maybe he's still in the hospital, locked away with Al in a "floor-flush" on some dark and stinking ward.

But then, at the window at night, having shuffled there as quietly as possible so as not to awaken my new roommates, peering down with my cheek pressed to the glass, close along the wall, I can see the ramp, oil stained and black where trucks have made their countless deliveries, there in the floodlights and leading away from the kitchen and storage areas at the rear of our wing, up through the narrow opening between the buildings to the street.

And I can't help but wonder if he made it. I have thought: I don't know him, this Monk, or for that matter any of these guys. In prison you never get to know a man because they move you, they split you up into different cellblocks or different facilities; they keep you from friendships the way they keep you from information—a man could use it against them. And so why should I care if Monk made it or not? What does it matter if he's four-pointed to a bunk or in Tahiti by now? What difference could it make to any of us still here in this hell hole?

I used to think that getting out of prison was the answer, that it would solve everything. I know better now. There's no way out of your head, not for Monk and not for me. The first couple of years I blamed my crime on my dad, the neighborhood I grew up in, the reformatory, drugs, even my genes. I was angry; I wanted out. I escaped via the sluice gate and got caught. I nearly went under the wall with Stansky and Lincoln, but changed my mind. But there is more than one way out, I figured. So I got my GED, then took college courses and got an associate's degree when they still had the Pell Grants, correspondence courses after that, and nearly all my free time reading books in the library—if not physically, I could do it in my head, I reasoned. But I was wrong. It took me ten years to realize I had shot that man and his daughter, that it wasn't drugs or my dad or the city streets; it was me. I shot them because I couldn't get what I wanted, and now every day I wish to God I hadn't; every day it's here in front of me and leaving prison won't make it go away—even though a piece of me wants Monk to make it, wants to be with him on that fantasy island in the Pacific.

Out in the hall there is a commotion. Midmorning, a week since Monk and the others disappeared, and there is a violent scuffling, no one shouting or screaming so I know it's serious—enough action that it's worth a trip on my walker to the door.

This hospital. Nothing shines. Not the floor, the walls, the glass, or the equipment; the bulbs seem dimmer somehow, as though the state has rationed electricity, and everywhere there is the pickled smell of disinfectant and dirty bedsheets. There are thirty rooms, ten to the left, along with the nurses' station and utility rooms, and twenty to the right, leading to the double security doors at the end of the ward. Moving into the hall from the last room—the same room I was in with Monk and Marty and Al last week—I can see the length of the aisle, the long, narrow shot of it crowded with laundry carts, janitor's carts, wheelchairs, a line of gurneys parked along the wall like a string of flatbed railroad cars, IV stands, the drug cart, food carts, soiled gowns and towels and sheets everywhere on the floor.

And now there are guards and nurses hurrying my way, frowning, weaving through the vehicles in the hall and turning quickly into a room halfway along the ward. The scuffling stops, and someone is yelling—one convict accusing another of stealing.

But nurse Camden suddenly appears from the room next door, followed by a new set of trainees. There are five this time, four females and a male, and not one of them turns to look in the direction of the commotion up the hall. Nurse Camden appears tired. Usually there is a bounce to her heavy-footed step, and usually her hair is drawn tightly into the bun at the back of her head, so that the corners of her eyes are stretched nearly into a smile. But this morning her hair is tucked loosely into her hat, and she is frowning, as everyone else seems to be around here; as she approaches she glares at me bent over in my walker, and I want to ask her what happened to Monk: Did he make it? Was it in the papers? On TV? And what about Marty and Al, what happened to them? Are they all right? Are we all going to be all right?

Instead, she stops in front of me. "This is Mr. Pitts," she says. The trainees line up next to her. The male feigns disinterest, but the females are nervously attentive. Nurse Camden points at my feet. "These are ankle cuffs. Mr. Pitts is here from a medium-security facility, which means he isn't tethered to his bed. As long as he's in his room at count and for feeding, and as long as he obeys the rules, we don't mind if he gets a little exercise in the hall." She studies my clothes, my frayed gown and beaten slippers. I can smell her now: soap, cigarettes, disinfectant, vomit, breath mint, omelet, coffee, sweat, sour milk—a roll call of her morning. She steps around me and moves into the room, scans the beds, the floor— checking, checking—then turns and walks to the window. She has never done this before—gone to the window, never put her hand on the sill nor leaned close with her face to the glass, peering down with her squinty-eyed stare toward the ramp below—and immediately I feel a tingling in my dead foot, a ghostly remnant that if I didn't know better I'd say was delight, a spontaneous desire to jump for joy.

"Mr. Pitts," she says to me, "I want you to stay away from this window. I want everyone to stay away from this window. It's against the rules, you know."

Knee High

It is the fourth of July. "Knee high by the Fourth of July." It is the Fourth of July and Dwight has just remembered what his father and maybe all of Iowa used to say about the corn in the fields. He could laugh, if his hip didn't hurt so much. The bullet is in there somewhere, lodged in his thigh or his groin—he is aware of a burning sensation in his lower gut, a pressure he has never felt before. Whoever said that when you are shot, there is no pain? Oh but the pain is everywhere, it never stops, it throbs with your heartbeat, and there are moments when it is unbearable, pain that rips the breath from your lungs, that leaves you wet and helpless and panting for life. He could laugh, the irony of it—"knee high by the Fourth of July"—here in a cornfield in Mexico, wounded and cowering like an animal, a million years from his childhood.

It was simple—he had embarrassed them. They were Federal police, *Policia Judicial Federal*, and he had taken their pride. It was a deal and they never delivered, a ton of seedless pot from Nayarit, but the burlap sacks in the truck were stuffed with hay. Except they didn't know him, they figured he was weak, a gringo with no heart, so he got a gun and went to their house and took his money back, two hundred thousand, U.S. It wasn't the money, or that he had surprised them—it was that he had gone too far with the gun, got caught up in the power of it. Dwight the joker, made them strip and hold each other's dicks, said things about their wives and mothers. So that he knew they'd kill him if they ever found him.

When you are afraid, you remember. It is Iowa and Dwight is twelve years old. A Sunday in late August and he has just come in from the fields with his father, all the relatives and Toni, his pretty thirteen-year-old cousin, there in the yard for the picnic, and everyone turns when his father says, "We'll get something out of this boy yet. What did you learn, son? Can you work the picker? Can you harvest the corn, boy?" And all Dwight can see is his cousin's white dress and how it clings to her thighs—all he can think about is tassels and silk, rows of sweet milky seeds in overripe husks—and with his hands in his pockets he blushes and nods and couldn't care less about the tractor or the picker or the silage in the barn.

Corn. Maize. A wild grass. *Gramineae*, genus *Zea*. Where does he remember this from? Except it is different here in Mexico. It is higher because it was planted earlier, but also it is papery thin, wilted, not at all like the corn in Iowa. Maize, common denominator of Latin America. Sacred plant of the Nahua and Aztec. *Masa* for tortillas. *Elote* dripping with chile and lime . . . and Dwight is in the Volkswagen, engine gasping for fuel, careening down the embankment into the field, plants toppling beneath the fenders, a quarter mile before he runs out of gas. . . .

The way things come around, the way everything turns in circles, coming back . . . it had been a year since he'd gone to the Federale's house and taken his money; a year and he'd tried a thousand times to convince himself it was over, they had forgotten, they'd never find him. But then the gas station at the *glorieta* Mariano Otero, the crowded *Pemex* noisy with cars and trucks, the black Ford pulling in three rows away. And Dwight, with the fuel hatch open and the cap off, the attendant standing dumfounded with the hose in his fist and not a drop of gas yet in the tank, Dwight starts the engine and idles quietly away from the pump. But it doesn't work; they see him, the Ford trapped in line now with a truck behind it, the men scrambling from the doors with guns drawn—and Dwight, hunched over, bullets popping all around him, his hip on fire, jams the accelerator to the floor, steers the groaning Volkswagen into the traffic at the *glorieta*.

The irony was, he had always considered himself prepared. On the road he was a master of disguise. Others had gone to planes and boats for the smuggle, but Dwight could move it on the ground, up through Mexico and over the border in anything with wheels. He'd started with travel trailers,

Airstreams, hollowed out the floors and packed them with *colitas*, hired retirees to drive the bridge at El Paso. And then there were trucks: pickups and vans, ten-wheel lorries, tanker trucks. And cars, always cars, standard tourist sedans, Buicks and Mercurys, Chryslers with giant trunks and no spare, souped-up engines and boosted CBs. And for his personal use in Guadalajara it was a Mexican Volkswagen with local plates, something invisible around town, to run errands in and not be noticed. And then—the irony of it—in a city choking with unnoticeable cars, in a *Pemex* packed with ordinary vehicles like his own—a coincidence, the cruelest of circles—the last people he wanted to be seen by, pull in and immediately spot him. And all the master of disguise has to save his life is his ordinary Volkswagen running on empty, a cornfield to hide in.

When you are alone, you try. Dwight the friendly one, the joker in school, the lover. His father and mother were dead— killed themselves drunk on a rainy night in a pick-up—and Dwight had moved in with his aunt and his cousin Toni. His aunt, following a boyfriend to Denver, rented a junky brick house on the West side, put Toni and Dwight in a city school. Toni was sixteen then, Dwight fifteen—Dwight with the smile, always with a joke to cover his loss—Dwight the lover, learning to coax her into it, always a story before she gave in. Every night they'd go at it, every Saturday and Sunday when her mother was hung over. They tried it all, Toni stealing the pill from her mother's closet, and later

Dwight breaking into neighbors' houses and even a drug-store for a fresh supply. They did it at home, they did it in cars and theaters, they said they were in love. But then after graduating Dwight fell in with a crowd—in high school you drink, you smoke pot, you deal a little; and then out of school, one day you're selling ounces, and next it's kilos. Dwight the joker, always a story, but with his new friends it was hard to keep up the front, and anyway Toni had grown older and already there were men where she worked. And it began to eat at him, this love for his cousin; it was unnatural how much he loved her—so that when the deal came he took it, Dwight the talker, Dwight in his twenties now with money in his pocket, on his way to Mexico with a used trailer and an address in Guadalajara.

The *glorieta* Mariano Otero. Another busy *Pemex* station, stinking of diesel fuel and cheap gas and *carnitas* boiled in fat. The black Ford three lanes over, and about the only lucky thing was the truck pulling in behind, boxing them in. So he had got away, ducked low in the seat while they shot at him, drove wild out Avenida Lopez Mateos changing lanes all the way to the *periférico*, down into the cornfield.

And when you are hurting, you long for what you had. He will never forget. It is January in Denver and he meets her on the sidewalk, and although she has not seen him for years she is not surprised. He tells her he still loves her, and she shakes her head. "Did you think I'd wait?" she says. "Did you expect that?" Toni outside her mother's house, slender legs in faded jeans below her bulky winter jacket, long blonde hair tucked snugly into her wool hat, sunglasses reflecting his face. She is on her way to work and she is not surprised. He begs her. He tells her lies he is no longer sure are lies. This is the way he is; mystery is his weapon, he can show up any-time, tell you lies until you give in, convince you he left for a reason. And Toni shivers a smile, her lips as young and inviting as ever. "Dwight, we were children. It's different now. We can't just pick up where we left off."

But they did, for a while. Toni was broke, waitressing year-round at minimum wage, saving what she could to ski during the winter months. So he took her to Albuquerque, rented a sprawling house in the suburbs, and bought her everything—furniture, a car, jewelry—mostly what she never had. And she believed the lies and laughed at his stories, and some of them came true—five Chryslers at a time, Guadalajara to Juarez, air shocks and no spare at a hundred miles per hour, passing trucks and buses like a squadron of fighter planes—the crossing at El Paso was a payoff, and then the cruise up the freeway to Albuquerque, five identical Chryslers to the house where Toni waited, one an hour into the garage, and the neighbors never flinched. A ton a trip, a quarter million dollars wholesale.

But you never stay in one place long, you never know if they're on to you. So he closed the house in Albuquerque, and Toni returned to Denver, waited for him, but when he didn't show she went back to work. It was six months before he finally caught up with her, and this time he took her to Mexico, rented a house on Lake Chapala where, despite their promises to each other, she got pregnant. Dwight working with new partners then, rodeo jocks from Texas hauling weed through a hole in the fence, bunch of good ol' boys in their daddys' trucks. Dwight with a million in cash, piles of it buried in the yard because he didn't know how to spend it. Toni said to him one day, "You're obsessed. Smuggling's worse than a drug for you; it blinds you to everything. You've got no home, no friends, you've got what?—ten different IDs? Dwight, you think you're free but you're not. You gave up everything. You gave up your *self*."

And then they lost the baby. Toni waking him one morning sobbing, half the sheet already soaked in blood. He couldn't move. He shouted for the maid, but when the old woman arrived in the bedroom she only shrieked and cupped her hands to her mouth. An hour's drive to the hospital in Guadalajara and he thought Toni wouldn't make it, Dwight crazy on the highway, the vision branded forever in his mind of the maid at the foot of the bed, wailing and holding as if in supplication the tiny fetus in her bloody hands. And Toni said in the hospital a week later, the day before she caught a plane back to Colorado, "No more, Dwight. I can't live this way. I can't carry your secrets."

But Dwight would see her from time to time, years later; show up at her job or her house unannounced—finally she moved to a town in the Rockies and bought herself a cabin, got married, and with her new husband opened a restaurant at a ski area—Toni afraid to look at him when he appeared at her door with another of his stories, but then—crazy as it was—she found him in his hotel room later, made love to him one last time. And every day he plays out the memory of her, scene after scene, of the two of them together, like a scratchy old film with no ending, nothing ever resolved.

Four, maybe five bullets have hit the car, and somehow he has made it around the *glorieta*—he is in the left lane, heading south on Lopez Mateos. His hip is on fire, and there are ragged holes in the door panel, chunks of vinyl on his lap and even across on the passenger's side. It is a Mexican Volkswagen, no power, the accelerator to the floor, and he is barely passing the traffic on his right—odd, he thinks, he has never noticed before, how time slows, how when you are desperate it is all less than real—cars and buildings, people on the sidewalks—everything fragmented by the light flashing through the trees, gliding by in slow motion.

At the intersection of the *periférico*, Dwight veers left in front of a traffic cop who blows his whistle and then gestures in disgust. The Volkswagen coughs, catches in second gear, and slowly accelerates. His chest, his shoulders ache now, and there are spasms of pain down his left leg—when he lifts his hand from his pants there is blood, and still he is surprised, even though he knows he has been shot. The engine sputters again . . . and he can't go on, he can't risk running out of gas on the highway, not where he can be seen. So he yanks the wheel and holds tight, careens off the blacktop and down the embankment, guns it into the field.

The corn is high but not high enough, and now he sees that it is not what he thought, not at all like the corn in Iowa. The rows are uneven, the soil is dry and hard; everywhere there are patches of stunted plants, some with gray, shriveled leaves and bamboo-like stalks. It is flour corn, the seeds soft and starchy, *masa* corn, corn that should be thick and ripe this time of year.

In first gear now, the Volkswagen digs sideways across a sandy area, bites, and lurches forward. Dwight heads for the far side of the field—there is a small village he remembers seeing from the highway, a few brick and adobe buildings where he might hide the car and find someone who will help. But the engine suddenly dies, chokes to life and then dies, and the car abruptly stops. He tries the starter. He opens the door and tries again, but it will not catch—the pain in his hip is unbearable now, and he has the impossible thought that he will have to walk, that his luck has run out.

He pulls himself out of the car. The corn in this spot is tall; the husks are fat and the tassels mature, but the leaves are curled and thin, the stalks flimsy. He pushes a plant aside . . . and sees . . . suddenly with the feeling that his past, his entire life, is contained in this one familiar moment . . . sees the black Ford on the highway, speeding by—he should have known they would track him this far, the insane way he was driving on Lopez Mateos, the cop at the intersection—they probably know where he once lived with Toni out this way, figured he was going home . . . but they are passing by, they have overlooked his tracks in the field, four men in the car and they have missed him. . . .

His pants are soggy with blood, the crotch and down the inside of both legs, his hip also. He has lost control of his bladder, he is numb there, the nerves are gone—except it is not urine that leaks from him, it is blood.

He stumbles and falls. He tries to stand but his legs are weak, he cannot get a foot under him. He pulls himself along in the direction of the village, his breath, his heart roaring in his head. The thought of dying slips in, but he forces it down, buries it with fear.

And he thinks about what he would do if Toni were waiting for him, if he arrived home and she saw him this way. He would put on a show, of course, make light of it while she fussed over him. But then later he'd weave it into a story, oh yes, make it something fantastic—a shootout with Interpol, the CIA, Dwight caught in a web of international intrigue. . . .

But Toni is gone. It has been years. The week she left, Dwight married a young Mexican girl he met in a bar, took her to the Yucatan, and bought a fleet of tourist boats. But he soon got bored with the job and with his new wife so he disappeared, never bothering to divorce her. And then in Chiapas in an Indian village during a drug buy he bought not only a load of weed but one of the daughters for sale, a dozen maidens displayed in the plaza and he picked one, fourteen years old and she couldn't even speak Spanish—a week later he gave her money and sent her home on a bus from Mexico City. So it wasn't as if there were no victims. Victims he had never met, victims he had slept with. Victims like Toni who would never tell anyone.

Dwight hears it: an engine, someone hard on the gas, and not on the highway but closer. And other sounds: tires spinning, the thumping, scraping noise of a car bottoming out in the dirt, plants snapping.

He struggles to one knee, grabs a stalk, and with his remaining strength manages to stand, balancing himself on the prop roots of the plant. The Volkswagen is only a few meters away, and in the same narrow swath it made through the corn from the highway, he sees the roof of the Ford, shiny black in the morning sun, diving, surging forward with the roar of the engine. They have come back. They saw him after all—they passed by only to taunt him, he thinks, only because they knew he was trapped. He must run. . . .

. . . But he is too weak. He sinks to his knees and looks at his pants. Blood is everywhere now. Knee high . . . he thinks, the Fourth of July. But the corn is different and this is not Iowa and when you are dying, what good does it do to remember?

He sits, and collapses to his side in the dirt. And he thinks . . . and he thinks: there must be a way, there must be something. He cannot escape, they will surround him. He can't play dead, they will shoot him anyway. The black Ford is behind the Volkswagen now, only yards away, and he cannot save himself—there is no way to stop it, no way out.

And it strikes him that he is too calm, that although he is about to die he is not as frightened as he should be; all he feels now is tired, so thoroughly exhausted.

And he thinks . . . that when they approach, when they circle around and glare at him, when they point their guns at his head and at his heart—at that timeless instant before they shoot . . . he will simply do what he has always done. He will smile. He will laugh. He will joke with them until they forgive him.

Or perhaps he will tell them a story.

Mel

It is late winter . . . sun high in a pale blue sky, the air sharp with the scent of pine from the foothills to the west. Mel has been driving for three hours, from her home on the western slope to this city on the edge of the plains where the mountains have become wrinkled fingers stretching eastward, dry escarpments hugging the river, and where the highway no longer meanders with the lay of the valley but abruptly widens to become a busy thoroughfare into town—immediately to the left is the prison: high stone walls and tin-roofed guard towers, chain-link fences topped with concertina wire, a parking lot out front.

She locks the car door. It is Saturday, visiting day, nearly noon, and there are plenty of vehicles in the lot. She is here to meet a man she does not know, a prisoner now for thirteen years. She does not know this man and yet she has carried the memory of his hooded face, his youthful and powerful hands, since the night he shot her father, shot her also, left her for dead. And she has carried the memory all these years, like the still tender scar at the base of her skull.

Mel fancies herself a vagabond, and rightfully so. She is also a writer, but of this she must frequently remind herself, even though she has had numerous articles and even a book published, with another on the way. It is that travel has been her release and writing her anchor, and with her fears, somehow she has equated success with being trapped, travel with freedom. Although now, for the first time in thirteen years, she has settled into one place in one town, and for the first time ever she is living with a man, someone she met while hitch-hiking in Mexico—his name is Hank and he is currently a ski instructor and a bartender at a resort near where they live, and he is in love with her. And this is why she is here—now that she has a home she is aware of a connection to this prison, to the man who possesses in his crime the greater part of her.

There is a solitary tower out front, a gate through a high fence, and a walkway leading to a sixties-modern building fronting the stone wall. Mel enters the building via glass doors and stops at a desk where a uniformed officer hands her a form to read—visiting rules—and another to fill out: name, address, driver's license number, name and number of inmate, relation to inmate. She does this quickly and hands it along with her driver's license to the officer. She knows the inmate's name—Alex Pitts—but because she does not know his penitentiary number the officer must find it on a list. As to "relation," she has written: friend.

Mel did not plan this visit. She is not sure what will happen. She knows that Alex Pitts is here—her brother in Omaha has checked every year for thirteen years to make certain—but she does not know if he has a family now, a wife or a girlfriend who visits him. She knows only that he was young when he arrived—eighteen, a year younger than she—and that he was a drug addict, a homeless boy with a record for burglary since he was ten.

She signs a waiver to be strip-searched, which a female officer tells her is a formality and to which she will probably not have to submit. Mel wears no jewelry and has never carried a purse, so there is nothing but her wallet to place in a nearby locker. She is dressed according to the rules—no short skirt or dress (Mel has not worn a dress in twenty years, since she was twelve and her father had to beg her to attend an Easter party with him), no tight or see-through blouses, no revealing sweaters—she wears what she usually wears: sweatshirt and jeans and sneakers, a jacket with pockets for her notebooks and pens, empty now. The guard pats her down and assists her through a metal detector, and suddenly she is on the other side of a steel door and in a barred sally port—inside the prison now—through another door and into a wide, rectangular room with cinder-block walls and a linoleum floor, square pillars supporting a cement ceiling, thirty or forty metal tables surrounded by folding chairs, a row of vending machines along one wall, and an old wooden desk in the corner, another uniformed guard behind it.

There are other people in the room—families, women alone—but no inmates, although Mel is not sure what an inmate looks like, what sort of outfit he wears. She finds an empty table against the wall, eases herself onto the chair, and scans the room. It is curious—she has never seen the races so thoroughly mixed—whites and blacks and Hispanics not in groups but scattered here and there in the room and even mingling at a row of tables that have been pushed together—even the waiting areas of bus and train stations, all the airports she has been in, are not like this.

A woman with yellow, straw-like hair and dreadfully thin arms, sitting alone at the next table, smiles tentatively at Mel and lifts a hand, wiggles her fingers in a half-hearted wave. "I haven't seen you before," she says, her face the face of a sad clown, pouty red lips and chalky skin, dark circles like sink holes around her languid brown eyes. "Did you bring quarters? You know, you can have quarters in here, for the machines." She opens her other hand and reveals a roll of coins. "I couldn't stand it here without a pop or a candy bar or something."

Mel nods and shrugs and can't think of anything to say. She has not brought quarters; nor does she drink pop or eat candy. Immediately the woman with straw hair is up and around her table and over to Mel's, where she sits across from her. "You here to see your father?" she says.

"My father?"

"Well, it can't be your husband or your brother, you're too

young. Haven't you heard? This is Old Max. They moved the youngsters out to the new prisons and brought the old-timers here, all the cripples and sick people because this is where the hospital is. Isn't that the perfect name . . . Old Max?" She lifts an eyebrow. "You really are new here. You wanna Coke or something?"

Mel is about to reply but the woman jumps up again. "Be back," she sings, heading for the vending machines. Not long ago Mel would have told this woman who is probably younger than she is and who hasn't the courtesy to wait for an answer that she wants to be alone, that No, she is not here to visit her father and for that matter it is none of her business, and anyway a Coke is about the last thing she needs right now—but the woman, as disheveled as she is in her shabby pink blouse and threadbare jeans and that crazy broom of yellow hair, has about her a toast-colored light, a pulsing aura of youthful warmth that follows her like a mist.

It is this that Mel sees. The year of recovery after the crime she had had a dream—that in removing herself from the pain she would sense what others could not, she would see differently; she would come to know and to trust people by their light. And slowly, over the years, with practice, the dream came true. So that what began as a nightmare has become for her not only a shield but a treasured advantage, a glimpse into the future, a head start.

It is a willful act, this seeing—she must allow her eyes to

drift out of focus; it is more a sensing, although the qualities
of vision are there: color, shape, density, the aspects of movement. And it is a talent she dares not reveal—Hank is the
only one who knows—for to tell someone, she is certain, is
to bring the sort of attention she most wants to avoid.

The woman returns towing her blob of tawny light; she
carries two cans of cola that appear as dark holes in her
glowing hands. She sits and tells Mel her name is Angie and
that, of course, she is here to visit her father . . . as she is every
weekend, three years now, back and forth from Colorado
Springs—God, the price of gas is killing her!, and now this
morning the car wouldn't start and she had to take a bus, a
bus mind you, and how will she get back?, there are no buses
until tonight, and she left her little girl with a neighbor so
she'll have to leave in an hour, probably have to hitchhike—
"say, you wouldn't be heading that way, would you?, I could
wait if you are!" . . . abruptly she tilts the can to her mouth
and gulps soda, eyeing Mel. When she finishes, she wipes
her mouth and smiles.

"Why is he here?" Mel says. "Your father."

"Because I put him here."

Mel waits in the silence that follows. She knows what is
coming next, although the words do not form in her head.

"He molested me," Angie says. "From the time I was five
until I was eighteen, when I got pregnant with his daughter.
But when he touched my baby girl, I called the cops."

Mel hasn't like canned soda since she can't remember

when, her teens, she supposes, but now she pulls the tab and lifts it to her mouth. The taste is familiar still, the icy bubbles a curious relief. "And you've forgiven him?" she says.

"Never. I have three brothers who hate his guts—they even hate me for coming here. No, no, we'll never forgive him. Who would?"

Mel feels that she has pried, for no good reason. Or perhaps there is a reason, but it is not obvious. Why is this girl sharing her wound? As though they were friends, compatriots.

Somewhere a metal door clangs, and there is the sound of heavy footsteps on the stairs, laughter, a shuffling as of cattle let out of a pen. And now they enter the visiting room, one at a time through a door in the corner next to the desk. The first is a tall black man with a matted gray beard, hurrying to a table of women with enormous smiles. Two more inmates enter—dark green slacks, green pullover shirts with the all-too-obvious number on the pocket—then more, a middle-aged man on crutches, another who must be in his seventies, stooped and frail but with a full head of bristly white hair, part of it braided into a rat's tail at the back of his head. Then Angie stands as the next man enters—he too is bent forward, and carries a cane, a large man with bulging arms and a long, sagging face. He smiles at Angie and Angie places her Coke on the table and winks at Mel. "That's my dad," she says—proudly, Mel thinks. "That's my dad."

Fifteen, twenty men have entered the room, and Alex Pitts is not among them. Mel waits another ten minutes and then finally approaches the officer at the desk who in turn telephones a control center somewhere in the prison. "You know how it is, lady," he says with his hand over the receiver, "some of these guys never get a visit, so they ain't ready."

Mel returns to her table next to the wall. She sits and wishes she had something to read, some way to calm the churning in her stomach. The tabletop has been etched with overlapping layers of graffiti, probably years of work. And with what? she wonders. What sharp instruments? Some of it is tattoo flash—snakes and dragons and devil's heads, skeletons and motorcycles—but most is another message: love, loved ones, hearts and arrows and who loves who; and dates: parole dates, release dates, who was here when.

Still, inmates are arriving. Two more enter the visiting room, and five minutes later, another two. A half hour has passed and Mel is beginning to think she should have handled this differently—she should have called the prison first, she should have written to Alex Pitts and told him she was coming. But she did not want him prepared for her, no more than she, thirteen years ago, was prepared for him. No, she tells herself, this meeting will be what it is—even if he does not show, for her it will be what it is.

The room is noisy. Half a dozen children have taken to the floor in a game of hide-and-seek, and the officer at the desk is frowning at them. Angie and her father are eating sandwiches purchased from the vending machines. Most of the inmates and visitors are smiling and talking and holding hands; except for the bars on the sally port and the heavy metal doors, it is a church social in a church basement. And out of the corner of her eye Mel sees the guard point his pencil at her—as she turns, another inmate enters the room.

He is younger than she expects, her age, but so much younger than the others. He is tall and powerfully built, with a narrow waist and wide shoulders—a build she does not remember—thick, sinewy arms filling the short sleeves of his green pullover. He is staring at her perplexed, now glancing self-consciously at the others in the room, then back at her, wondering. She does not recognize this man— the wide brow, the long and slightly crooked nose, the angular jaw—certainly not from the night long ago when he wore a mask, but not even from the news photos or the mug shots she saw months later at her brother's house, during the court proceedings. She had gone to the sentencing—a plea bargain to avoid the death penalty—in a wheelchair, still too weak to carry herself, but she had arrived late, nearly an hour after it was over, and they had taken him back to his jail cell where she could not see him, could not look into his eyes and glimpse there the knowledge of his future, the suffering that would never be enough. Because it is the eyes she remembers—blue, with flecks of gray, the color of winter sky, but framed, made violent by the mask holes, huge and desperate.

The same eyes, only softer now, questioning. Mel stands.

She must force herself to keep her hands apart, to keep from picking at herself like a bird. He looks back at the guard who has not moved, still with his elbows on the desk, hands folded, pencil dangling from his fingers, pointing at Mel. So he turns and walks up to her.

It was a foolish thing to say. She will think later, driving home, that it was dumb, silly. "I didn't bring quarters," she says. "I can't buy you anything from the machines"—Mel who is quick but who rarely speaks before thinking, who is ahead of possibilities.

He does not talk. She knows this, she has known it all along, since before the sentencing when her brother discovered that the man who shot his father and his sister could not talk, had not talked since childhood.

And now she wishes she had her notebook with her, a pen, although she supposes these items are not allowed in the visiting room. He is questioning her with his eyes, saying Who are you?, What do you want? But then he tenses and she knows he has just now figured it out, has recognized her. He blinks and clenches his jaw in a controlled expression of pain and surprise that says God!, and Why?

Mel sits. She reminds herself that she is not here for revenge—she cannot erase the memory, or the fear, but she is not here to vent an anger she long ago buried. She has come here to finish what she has begun herself—to untie this knot in her head—although she is not sure how this will happen, or even if she is right to try.

His face is tanned, clean-shaven, and there is a faint odor of soap about him. Unlike the other inmates he has no tattoos she can see, no scars. His hair is dark and straight, combed back. His wrinkles are sun wrinkles; he has the leathery skin of a man who has labored outdoors for years. And those eyes—blue, and too easily read, studying her.

"You're Alex," she says. "You shot me. You killed my father and then tried to kill me."

He sits across from her, wary, on the edge of the chair. He does not seem to know what to do with his hands.

He had got in through a window in the basement, crept up the service stairs and into her bedroom, woke her by shoving a gun in her mouth. Then marched her to her father's room and forced them both to lie on the floor, tied their hands and feet. The safe—Mel will never forget—the note held to her face, the childish scribble on paper torn from a school notebook— Where was the safe and what was the combination? But there was no safe, there was never a safe in the house, and her father told him, pleaded with this man who would not believe them, who ransacked the house, tore the paintings off the walls and toppled the dressers, emptied the closets and returned in a rage, wild-eyed and shaking—and shot them. Killed her father with a bullet to the head, there, next to her on the rug, murdered him. Then aimed the gun at her hair as she turned, the final instant, the endless hollow roar. . . .

". . . Wait," Mel says. She stands and walks to the desk, asks the officer for a pencil and paper. The guard grunts and hands her his pencil and opens a drawer, finds a sheet from a notepad. She returns to the table where Alex Pitts sits with his shoulders hunched, arms on the table, perfectly still. "Here," she says, placing the paper and pencil before him.

But he does not write. He looks at her with his winter blue eyes, the long lashes beneath thick, sunbathed brows. His jaw is square, his chin strong, and yet his mouth is small and moist, nearly heart-shaped, which lends a boyish and oddly vulnerable look to his face. His eyes are worried.

"You're on the labor gang, aren't you?" Mel says. "Is that why they keep you here, to do the jobs the old prisoners can't? Because they need you? You went to school, you took college courses and earned your degree, you've been here thirteen years and have only one report. That's pretty good, isn't it! . . . " She sits straight in her chair, feels an urge to clear her throat, but does not. ". . . Look, I know a lot about you from my brother. He calls here to check. You can understand that, can't you?"

But Alex Pitts does not answer. His body is as rigid as hers was the night he shot her. He is even beginning to tremble, ever so slightly, a nervous hand on the table.

The police had caught him in another house, a block away. A house with a safe. Melody had come to in a drying pool of blood, inched her way to the telephone, and managed with her teeth to pull the old metal phone off her father's roll-top desk. The man with the ski mask—Alex Pitts—had fired the gun into her hair, her wild, curly hair, just as she had turned—and had wounded her, the bullet taking a piece of her skull but leaving her alive. And all because, as the police would tell her brother weeks later, a crazy kid, a drug addict named Alex Pitts, had mistaken her father's house for another. Had shot them because he was frightened and sick and maybe didn't know any better.

She sighs. "I didn't come here for this, to convict you again. But I have to tell you what it's like for me. You changed my life. I can't say you ruined it because that's up to me, but you hurt me beyond measure. Do you see that?" Mel catches herself staring at him, tapping her knuckles on the table. "Right now I'm not sure why I'm here. I don't know you. I don't know if you feel bad about what you've done, but by the look in your eyes I'd say you do . . . after all, you could have left, you could have walked out of the visiting room the moment you realized who I was."

Alex Pitts lowers his gaze. He exhales through his mouth. It is the first time Mel has noticed him breathe.

"Why did you shoot us? Were you frightened? Desperate? Did you care that little for life? Were we like dust to you, something you could brush off your sleeve? Am I still that to you?"

There it is again, a shiver, that nearly imperceptible trembling of the hand.

"I want to know why." Mel picks up the pencil and holds it out to him. "You owe this to me. Tell me why you shot us. I don't care if it's not enough. I want to know what you were thinking. I want to know why I'm the way I am today." She waits, holding the pencil . . . a second, five seconds . . . then finally withdraws it. "Don't you realize?" she says. "What you did happens to me every day, and in a sense, what I do, what becomes of me, happens to you now. Doesn't that mean anything to you?

"Or is this your power? Was that why? Was it my loss and your gain? You shot me, so you own me, the rest of my life?"

She leans forward on the table, close to him now, as if to reveal a secret.

"Then let me tell you what you bought. Thirteen years, and I had no home and no friends, because possessions and relationships can be merciless, when they're taken away. I had nightmares. I saw things. Sometimes hooded faces with eyes like yours. I saw all sorts of things, like auras and halos and even events before they happened. For years I was afraid most of the time. I had this idea, as crazy as it sounds, that I was worth shooting. That no matter what I did or who I became, I should be punished. So I compensated—sometimes I was cruel, usually I was blunt, unforgiving. Does any of that sound right to you? Is that what you wanted?"

But Alex Pitts does not respond. He sits there, looking at her, hardly breathing. He should leave, she thinks. Why doesn't he leave? A chorus of "Happy Birthday" begins at a table in the center of the room. The old prisoner with white hair flamboyantly opens a bag of popcorn and dumps it on the table, and everyone cheers and claps. The sound echoes off the walls and ceiling, reverberates in the sterile air above her head. Mel feels herself dwindling, once again folding into herself, losing her sense of time and space.

But then across the room she sees Angie and her father rise, hug for a second, and make their way toward the door. Suddenly Mel wants out; she is tired of feeling trapped, she knows in her heart she was wrong: that the power was never his, was hers all along. She feels ridiculous, for trying, for talking to this man, for even coming here. She also has an urge to cry, something she has not done since before the crime.

She stands, steadies herself for a moment—she is light-headed, sweating now—and walks to the desk, asks the guard where the bathrooms are. On her way she stops and tells Angie to wait—not to hitchhike, please don't hitchhike, she'll be glad to drive her home—and then finds the women's room where at the sink she runs cold water on her wrists, cups her hands, and splashes it on her cheeks, her neck. But this time when she looks in the mirror she is no longer worried; she is certain she will no longer see there a face from the past, unchanged, the face in the mirror at her father's house all those years ago. Still Melody.

In the visiting room again Mel walks directly to the table to tell Alex Pitts she is leaving, but as she arrives she sees he has written something on the paper. He is hunched over the note, as if contemplating it, but then he slowly pushes himself up from the table and crumples the note in his hand. When he looks at her, there are tears in his eyes. He lingers a second, then starts across the room. At the desk he hands the pencil to the guard, and as he turns for the door Mel sees his light—a shimmer of blue, clear and close to the body, but wispy, flickering, as though starved for fuel, a pale blue flame in the wind—and then he is gone, through the door and into the interior of the prison. Mel looks at the guard who shrugs as if to say, "You know how it is, lady," and then she joins Angie who waits for her at the entrance to the sally port.

Outside, Mel and Angie are silent as they walk to the parking lot. The sky is cloudless, the sun high and unusually brilliant in the crisp air above the prison. It is a winter day, cold and fixed, and yet there is a hint of spring in this light, a fragile notion.

Acknowledgments

Thank you Bill, Karen, and Oreada for the opportunities and encouragement. For your loyal friendship year after year in the joint—Miles, Woody, Walt, Dave, Ken, Jeff, and so many others— I owe you. For the unconditional love from my soul friends Maurice and Joe on the streets, my eternal gratitude.

Special thanks to my agent Sam Stoloff at Frances Goldin Literary Agency for his tireless efforts and excellent suggestions. And to Tina Pohlman, my editor at Carroll & Graf, for believing in this book and for making it right. Also to Bell Chevigny, whose kindness and direction gave this project new life. I am much obliged.

And finally, for always being there, in every way, thank you Fr. Bob—you knew me when.

About the Author

J. C. Amberchele was born in Philadelphia in 1940 and attended a Quaker school, then colleges in Pennsylvania and New York, earning a B.A. in psychology. His fiction has been published in *Quarterly West, Writer's Forum, Blue Mesa Review, Portland Review, Oasis,* and *Doing Time: 25 Years of Prison Writing,* and two of his stories were awarded first prize in the annual PEN Prison Writing Contest. He is currently serving time in prison.

All of the author's proceeds from the sale of this book will be donated to the National Organization for Victims Assistance and The Osborne Association.